# RAESH

## A House of Ausher Novella

# EMBER DRAKE

RAESH

# Content/Trigger Warning

In Raesh, we follow the journey of a young male Andr (dragon) and how his life changed after he hatched and someone sold him into slavery. There are elements of violence and scenes of sexual assault in this story, as well as scenes of torture and the brief description of the assault of a minor.

# CHAPTER 1

Sang's movements were sluggish with the sun beating down on his bare back as he was dragged through cobblestone streets in chains. He lifted his head as high as he could manage to look around. The structures were large, with sloping, scalloped tops painted in gold. The red and gray painted stone walls were high with red lanterns along the walls in the square holes. He found them to be pretty. Sang watched as people milled about and gathered near the platform that he and several others were being shepherded on. He was the smallest of the group, and they had placed him in the middle, but those ahead of him pulled him forward, causing those behind him to bump into him. He moved too slowly for their liking.

None of them were there of their own will. Sang wondered if they had been tricked as well. His skin screamed as if it were on fire where the shackles clasped around his small wrists were. Blistering welts were forming where it had turned red. The pain was unbearable, and he was weak from hunger. His throat was dry, and his tongue felt like weighted wool in his mouth. It was far too hot.

A woman gasped, and chains rattled when a loud thud hit the platform. Those behind him groaned as they pulled their connected chains closer to them, and those that were ahead of him stumbled backward before catching themselves. Men in light armor jumped up onto the platform to pick up the boy that had fallen. He did not look to be more than ten years of age, but they had their swords at the ready as they chattered nervously to each other. The boy was small, but they had received a warning about him. He had small patches of black scales that had a green tint to them in various places on his body, but the ones that caught their attention were the long line of ornate armored scales that ran down his spine. They looked like rare gems encrusted with shiny emerald flecks, and smaller, gem encrusted scales surround each one.

The scales that lined the boy's spine shifted in size and shape, and the two larger ones in the center had long, thick bones grew out from their sides like a pair of arms and legs. The boy's pale skin turned bright red as two sets of black feathered wings shot out of the extended bones and his back in a spray of blood, covering the men and those chained directly in front of and behind him. Just as quickly as the wings appeared, the scale above his tailbone had shifted so that the parts that looked like curved pincers spread out and grew as a long, double-ended, ax-bladed tail shot out from beneath it. The bladed end immediately cut the armored man nearest to the boy's back in half, and his body burned to ash by one of the four balls of green fire that ran along the thick, black tail.

Panicked screams rose throughout the crowd as the boy struggled to his bare feet, his eyes glowing an eerie white. Those chained to him did their best to back away, but their movement had attracted the boy's attention, and he snarled as he moved to attack, but fell to his knees and let out an ear-piercing screech. He turned to see a long steel blade had been driven through his tail and into the platform. Before the boy could react, his eyes went wide, and his scream came out garbled as blood poured from his mouth. Blades had pierced his throat and chest. The boy collapsed to the side as his body turned a brighter red before catching fire. The bright green blaze caught those who were chained to his immediate front and back, reducing them to ash in moments along with the boy. Only a husk, resembling the boy, remained.

After a short time, observers noticed movement in the large pile of burned wood and ashes. The small boy-shaped husk began to crack and splinter off in pieces, revealing pale flesh beneath it bit by bit. The audience that reformed around what remained of the platform looked on as the remains of the ashen husk fell apart completely to show the nearly unmarred skin of the boy that had died there just moments before. His small wrists had scars around them where the manacles that bound him remained, continuing to sear his tender flesh.

The boy sat up slowly and looked around, wincing as he did so, to see that he was being stared at with a mix of shock and awe. His wrists still hurt badly, as the shackles did not burn away like the swords had done. Confusion lingered as he wondered how he stayed alive despite being certain that his body had burned away. It was not the first time that it had happened, but it was still a source of worry and confusion for him. He wanted to ask what he was and what was happening to him, but he did not speak the language of the new land he was in, nor did he understand it. The only words he recognized were Pak Sang Yong and Andr, but only because he had heard them repeatedly when they were talking about him. He knew one as his given name, but the other one was unfamiliar to him. He wondered what Andr meant and why people were afraid of him or elated when they saw him.

The travel from where he came from was long to where he was currently, but the people had similar features. The people in the new land held themselves differently and had different clothes. They did not seem any friendlier, though he knew kind people where he came from. At least he thought they were kind until he woke up one day in chains that burned him and in a place he did not recognize and around people that he did not know. Still, he tried to make the best of his situation. Those around him spoke the same language that he had learned at the very least. Once he thought they were not as afraid of him, he asked what he was and why he was so different, but none of them would answer him. So, he kept to himself after that. He got the feeling that there were more people that were afraid of him than happy to see him. Though the ones that looked happy to see him always had a hint of darkness in their eyes that he did not care for.

Sang, as he was called, felt a sharp sting across his face that brought him out of his memories and back to the audience staring at him still. A man in light armor was yelling at him, but he did not understand what was being said or why he was being yelled at. Probably for damaging the platform and killing people. He felt bad about it all, but there was really nothing he could do about it. He would have to accept any punishment that was given. Standing and readying himself for whatever they were going to do, a finely dressed, slender man shouted at what Sang thought was likely a guard. The finely dressed man shook a large and ornate bag in the air so the guard could see. It looked full and heavy. Another finely dressed man also shook a large, heavy bag at the guard, smiling wickedly at the other man, who was now frowning, his thinly mustached lip curling up in a sneer. The sneering, finely dressed man held up a second large bag, which made the other man's face scrunch up in anger. The situation puzzled Sang. His head went back and forth between the finely dressed men as they shouted at the equally confused guard, all while pulling bags that clinked and jingled from their belts.

The man that had brought Sang and the other captives to the new land had stepped in front of the two men. He was smiling broadly and Sang could see that same darkness in his eyes that got him into his current situation. He still did not like that look. It was one of greed and malice. Sang's already empty stomach hollowed and dropped, and he squirmed under the man's gaze. Something bad was happening.

As quietly as he could, Sang tried to move away from the distracted guard, but the other captives and the rattling of the chains gave him away. He now had the guard's full attention, and he was snatched up by his long hair. The man that put him and the others in chains walked away from the finely dressed men, one of whom was storming off, and came to Sang with a key in his hand. He unlocked the part that connected Sang to the others and then walked back towards the remaining finely dressed man after speaking to the guard. They forcefully dragged Sang by his hair off what remained of the platform and brought him to the finely dressed man. The finely dressed man smiled down at him, and Sang saw a different darkness in his eyes. It was not one of greed or malice. He was not sure what it was, but he knew it had to be bad. Another guard, accompanying the finely dressed man, took possession of him, and he struggled in his chains. The second guard took Sang by his chains with a look of sadness in his eyes. Sang did not understand the sadness, but it was becoming clear that he was not going to a good place.

# CHAPTER 2

T he room they kept him in had no light. It was always dark. He was grateful that he could see in the darkness, not that it mattered. He had no one and nothing to play with. Several days had passed since the finely dressed man brought him to his home. At least it felt like several days. They barely gave him food or water. It was only ever enough to keep him alive.

He saw two children as they brought him in. The children looked to be around his age, a boy and a girl. They only allowed Sang to have contact with the boy, but never let him play. They were both taught how to read and write, but Sang struggled because he did not yet know the language. During their lessons, if the other boy, Zi Han, performed poorly or misbehaved, the teacher would strike Sang with a stick or subject him to even worse punishments. When they were home, the same would occur and he would be thrown into his dark stone room.

The worst of his abuse came in the dead of night, when the house was asleep, and the guards patrolled the grounds. Leung Guo, the finely dressed man that bought him, would come to retrieve Sang from his room and take him to a much nicer one that was hidden away. There, Sang received sweets and wine to enjoy, but after a few nights, he stopped enjoying them. The wine was sweet, but it made him feel numb and sleepy. While he ate and drank, Leung would rub him all over. He, too, would partake in the drinking of wine. Sang assumed it was his way of showing him it was safe to drink.

The drinking and rubbing would continue for a while longer before Leung would put his mouth on various places of Sang's body. Sang would push him away when he touched his groin, and Leung would strike him across the face, then resume his rubbing and the removal of his clothes. As Sang was being laid down, he would feel the room spinning and subsequently lose consciousness. When he woke back up, he was back in his room on his thread-bear pallet, and the night had been swallowed by the day.

The following day, his body and head would ache, which was made worse when someone dragged him out of the comforting darkness of his room and into the harsh light of the sun to attend the day's lesson with Zi Han. Zi Han would always notice Sang's pain and deliberately shout in his ears. One day, Sang lashed out at Zi Han, leaving the boy with a visible mark on his face. When Leung saw it, he summoned a bolt of lightning and directed it at Sang. His whole body seized up, and he fell to the ground, bleeding. Guards picked him up and threw him into his room. They removed his pallet and left him there to bleed, but it was not too bad of a wound, and it slowly stitched itself back together. The only good thing that came out of it was that Leung did not come for him that night.

Later that evening, Sang could hear faint sounds outside. The far wall of his room faced the outside, and he always heard Zi Han and his sister playing or fighting. However, the sounds he was hearing were not of children, but the muffled sounds of a guard falling to the ground, and then another. Not long after, he heard the sounds of the lock on his door being messed with.

When the door opened, he could barely make out a figure coming toward him. Sang backed away, and the figure stopped moving forward before his head slid off his neck and rolled over to Sang. The sound of a blade being sheathed followed. The guard that had beheaded the intruder called for others to come and get the body. Once the body was gone, leaving a bloody trail from the smell and sound of it, Sang was once again left alone.

The following day, the guards acted as if nothing had happened, but Sang had overheard one of them say that Leung's rival had sent someone to steal the Andr and that Leung sent the dog's head and body back to his master. Sang knew what the Andr was, it was him, but he still did not know what exactly an Andr was or why someone would want to steal him. The person who came to steal him had an odd smell that Sang did not recognize, which differed from Leung's guards. None of them smelled like there were normal humans.

Sang knew Leung and his family were not normal humans either. Leung and Zi Han were both lightning elementals, but Leung's daughter, Xiao Mei, did not display such abilities. Sang supposed that she took after her mother and was just an ordinary witch. Whenever Sang could leave his room outside of lessons and abuse, he would observe Leung's excellent treatment towards his wife. Sang often wondered if she was aware of her husband's late-night activities while she was asleep. Not that it mattered. They were nobles, and he was sure that they paid the guards and staff well enough to ensure their silence regarding such matters. Sang's training made him able to move without being seen or heard, ensuring that he was truly on his own. The fresh brand on the back of his neck ached with the thought.

They had been out at sea, lost and off course, for days now. A storm had hit out of nowhere and took them into an unfamiliar part of the sea. There was no land in sight, and they were already low on provisions. They also suffered some injuries and casualties. They gave the dead a proper send-off before throwing them overboard.

Things were looking grim for the crew of the Pale Emperor. The captain, Ivy Thatch, was barely holding them all together. Her Valravn had flown out to find land and had yet to return. They needed food and medicine, and there were no other ships insight.

Ivy leaned over the side of her ship and sighed. Her stomach rumbled with hunger, but her crew came first, and if they did not eat, neither did she.

"Mermaids! Starboard bow!" someone called out.

She looked up and crossed over to the right side of the ship, and sure enough, there was a pod of mermaids swimming along the side of the ship. They were flirting with the food and attention starved men, trying to lure them into the water.

"Hey! Knock it off!" Ivy shouted at the mermaids. "I need all of my men alive. Now, fuck off before fish gets put on the menu."

The mermaids giggled and swam off. The men groaned and went back to their duties.

Again, Ivy sighed and leaned over the side. Something good needed to happen for them, and soon. Tempers were short enough, add hunger to the equation, and they would soon be at each other's throats. She wondered what grilled mermaid meat tasted like and would eating one make them cannibals? Just when she was about to walk away, one mermaid came back and called out to her.

"Sorry, but I prefer the company of warm-blooded men in my bed," said Ivy.

The mermaid laughed. "How bold of you to assume I wanted you in mine."

Ivy knitted her brow in confusion. Did merfolk sleep in beds? What did they cover themselves with? She shook the strange thoughts from her head before addressing the mermaid again. "What do you want?"

"No need to be so mean. I just came to help, but if you don't want my help, I'll gladly leave," she said, treading water, letting the ship slowly go past her.

Ivy narrowed her eyes at the fish woman. "What could you possibly have that could help us?"

"Apologize for being so rude and then I'll tell you." She smiled, baring her shark-like teeth.

Ivy rolled her eyes and sighed with exasperation. "Fine, sorry."

The mermaid pouted. "Like you mean it."

Ivy glared down at her. "Swim away, little fish," she said, turning to walk away.

"All right!" the mermaid called out. "I'll tell you."

Ivy smiled to herself, straightening her face before facing the mermaid. "All right. Out with it, then." She added, "Please," politely, getting a smirk from the mermaid.

"We saw a ship close to here," she offered.

Ivy perked up. "What kind of ship?" Another ship would be a boon if it were the right kind.

"Not sure," she shrugged. "It was as big as yours and had lots of tasty-looking men on it," she purred. "Oh, and it smelled of spice and other meats."

Food! They had food! But the ship was as large as the Emperor and likely armed. Her crew was in no shape for a fight, but the prospect of a good meal might give them the strength that they would need to take the other ship.

"Where?" Ivy asked. "Where is this other ship?"

"Now, now, I can't just tell you without some sort of payment. Like you humans all say."

Ivy glared again. "What do you want in exchange for the location of this supposed other ship? And don't ask for the flesh of my men," she warned.

Again, the mermaid pouted. "Fine, the other ship was mean to us, anyway. When you take the ship, you give us some of their men."

"Deal!" Ivy agreed. "Now, where is it?"

"Just follow me this way," she said, pointing behind her.

Ivy looked the girl over. She was beautiful, as mermaids tended to be. She had long, wavy red hair and bright blue eyes with full pouting lips. Since mermaids could rarely be trusted, she had no way of knowing if they were being led into a trap. There was a fair-sized bounty out for Ivy and the crew of the Pale Emperor. They had a reputation for wrecking other ships and killing their crews, but they only did so when necessary. Crew deaths only happened when the King of Tides ordered it. She never knew his reasons, only that he was a sadistic bastard.

"How do I know you're not playing us?" Ivy asked. Hungry or not, she would not lead her crew to being captured or to their deaths.

The mermaid smiled broadly up at her. "You're just going to have to trust me."

"Well, I don't," Ivy replied. "Give me a reason."

"They tried to kill us; we owe that crew nothing. "We're hungry, too," she spat angrily. "We would be helping each other."

"All right, but you're going to have to earn your meal. Help us by luring them to us and you can have as many of their crew as you can eat," Ivy offered. She did not like offering up the lives of others, but it was for the sake of her crew.

The mermaid frowned, but nodded her agreement, then swam off in the direction she pointed out.

Ivy called out to the helmsman, instructing him to follow the mermaid, and informed the others to prepare for boarding another ship that potentially had food and medicine for those who had fallen ill during their time of being lost at sea. Her crew cheered at the possibility of getting food that had not gone stale. Ivy prayed to whatever god was listening to help them in their success. She did not really believe in any, but she had to believe that something was looking out for them to have sent mermaids and what was likely a merchant ship. Now, if they could find a port when they were done, that would be fantastic.

It nearly took half the rest of the day before they finally spotted the other ship. Ivy did not need a spyglass to see it, though. Her right eye possessed a magical enhancement that allowed her to see a long distance away. From what she could see, the ship was an East Indiaman and belonged to the East India Company. They had to be careful with their approach to the enemy vessel. Ivy gave the order to fly friendly colors and act as if they were in distress. Technically, they were in distress; they had sick and wounded aboard, but the merchant vessel did not need to know all that. They just needed to be in range of the Emperor's cannons. The mermaids did as asked and got the vessel to sail closer to assist them.

Considering who the ship belonged to, they could leave no survivors. The East India Company did not take well to pirates or having their ships looted. The crew of the Pale Emperor did not need word getting back to the company for what they were about to do. They would need to sink the ship as well. The mermaids would eat well that evening, and so would her crew if the mermaid's sense of smell was anything to go off of. Once the ship was in range, Ivy gave the order to raise the bloody colors, the flag that meant certain death for the other ship, and to fire on their rigging. The last thing they needed was for their meal to get away.

Ivy had her men grapple over to the other ship so they could pull the ships together for easier boarding. With the red flag raised, she had a line of riflemen at the ready to prevent the hooks from being dislodged or having the ropes cut. When they boarded, the opposing crew lined up on their knees, clasping their hands behind their heads. Some of them were crying and begging for their lives. The only one still standing was most likely the ship's captain. He had his logbook in hand and asked for mercy. Ivy wanted to consider it. She could use more tradesmen that knew their way around a ship, especially after she lost some to that storm, but these men did not look like much and would not make good deckhands, let alone pirates. Besides, she promised the mermaids their share of the take. She would recruit more when they found a friendly port.

With the ship secured, Ivy went to inspect the cargo in the hold as she went over the ship's log. At least she had a vague idea of where they were, the Indian Ocean from the looks of the last ports that were logged. The logbook would be useful in getting their bearings and finally making port. They would have something of value to trade, and her crew could get some much-needed rest and a little recreation. The reliability of the mermaids pleasantly surprised her. There was indeed spice and various dried meats on board. How they could smell it all was strange though, but the how did not matter now. Her crew would eat well for a while, and they could sell the rest. Perhaps there were gods, after all.

# CHAPTER 3

H e ran. Sang did not know where he was going, but he knew he had to get as far away from where he was as he could. He was bleeding badly from his left shoulder, but he could not stop running. If they caught him, they would punish him again. So, he ran.

Sang stumbled, barely catching himself with blurred vision from the loss of blood, but he could hear people yelling behind him as he passed by. Mostly drunks and vagrants at such a late hour. Running was not helping him. He needed to hide now. At least until he could get the bleeding to stop. He ducked down an alley and staggered as far back as he could before he collapsed.

Sang was not sure how much time had passed, but when he opened his eyes again, he saw the face of a boy not much younger than him. He looked to be around fifteen years old. Sang felt hot all over, as if his skin was burning. When the boy recoiled from touching him as if he had been burned, Sang reacted by grabbing the boy and tearing into his throat. He did not understand why he suddenly bit the boy.

The boy's blood was warm as it entered Sang's mouth, and it tasted like metal before becoming gritty as it traveled down his throat. It felt like he was swallowing dirt and small stones that he had to chew, but he only wanted more. Though he was younger, the boy was bigger than Sang, stronger looking, and he struggled in his hold. Before it turned to metallic dirt and stones, it was sweet and fiery, and he could feel his strength coming back to him. Sang held the boy tighter. Soon, the boy went limp in his arms, and then he went cold.

Sang quickly dropped the boy and backed away. It was then that he realized that the wound on his shoulder had knitted itself back together and healed completely. He had taken a lightning bolt to his shoulder as he rejected his master's predatory advances once again. This time Sang fought back and injured the old man, which caused him to be struck with the statically charged air as he ran away.

Tentatively, he went back over to the lifeless body of the boy and lightly touched it, wishing it would go away. As soon as he put his hand on the body, it lit up in a bright green flame that quickly devoured the body whole. Sang got up and hurriedly got out of the alley as the buildings that it sat between caught fire. He looked down at his small hands and their long, thin fingers, with wide eyes as he backed away from the blaze.

Sang stood in awe as he watched the fire consume the buildings. Panicked screams filled his ears as people ran about, many trying to put the blazing flames out but having no success. Others were looking for any way into the buildings to see if there were people trapped inside. He continued to back away from the horrific scene, and when he turned around to run away, he ran into a man in a lightly armored uniform. Sang hit the ground hard; he was small and frail for his eighteen years. Sang's master and family subjected him to frequent starvation and beatings for no reason. He was a slave, after all.

Before he could get to his feet, the guard snatched him up.

"Did you do this?" the guard asked.

Sang shook his head and babbled incoherently. He did not know what exactly happened or how.

The guard looked him over and narrowed his eyes. The boy in his hands was thin and strange looking, with patches of scales around his hairline. He roughly turned the boy around and moved his hair aside, revealing the scar of a brand on the back of his neck.

"You're the pet Leung is looking for," he smiled viciously, turning the boy back around to face him. "You're coming with me, boy. Your master will pay handsomely for your return."

Sang lay on the cold stone floor of his room, curled in a ball. Naked and shivering, but otherwise unable to move. His long, black hair, slick with sweat and blood, was his only cover over his pale skin. They brought him back to the house of Leung and subjected him to a severe beating. After the beating, they forcibly ripped off four of the large, bejeweled armored plates down his back. They were the only protection he had on his body, and they were the main reason he was being kept alive. At least that was what he believed to be true.

To stop the bleeding, they struck him with multiple lightning bolts, since fire had no effect on him. Fire was not much of a weapon against an Andr. He had never met others like him, and his master would not tell him anything more than that he was what was called an Andr. A dragon in human form.

He knew he would heal, eventually—he always did—with rest and hopefully some food. They took two of the scales as payment for the damage to the thankfully empty buildings. They paid the guard who found him and brought him back with another scale, and they took one for the life of the boy he killed. As punishment for escaping, they once again took away his pallet. He did not know how he could heal so quickly before, but he knew he wanted more blood. And he would get more as soon as he healed and escaped again.

# CHAPTER 4

His wrists hurt, but he was grateful that his chains were not the kind that left burns. He was also grateful that they were easy to get out of. They had chained Sang up in his room for attempting to escape again. They once again beat him for it, but he would not stop. At least he got to keep his pallet this time, and Leung had stopped coming for him. Sang noticed the cries of another young boy close by.

He thought about setting the boy free, but it was hard enough getting out on his own. So, he left him there. Sang crept into the main part of the house, dodging the guards. He had memorized their patrols, which made getting out a matter of good timing on his part. Once he got past the guards, he slipped upstairs. He was still weak from his last beating. He required blood just in case he had to fight.

Sang skipped past Xiao Mei's room and headed straight for Zi Han's room. Even at eighteen, the boy was a pain, and Sang hated being his stand-in for the whip whenever Zi Han purposefully did something wrong. Xiao Mei was also a menace and just as cruel to Sang as her mother was, but Leung and Zi Han were the worst. They had a room built with large bells that made Sang's skin itch when he got too close. They would lock him in the room for hours and ring the bells until his ears bled, but they always stopped when he passed out and his skin turned red. Zi Han's blood would probably be bitter, but it would be worth it to watch the lights fade in his eyes. He would take it all.

As quietly as he could manage, Sang entered Zi Han's room. The young man was fast asleep with a woman in his bed curled around him. Sang cursed internally. He had not planned on there being someone else in the room. The thought crossed his mind to go back, but he would not give up. He would have his freedom. No matter the cost.

Sang moved closer to Zi Han's bed, carefully stepping over anything that would alert Zi Han, the woman, or the guards to his presence there. He hovered over Zi Han for a few moments. The boy looked so peaceful as he slept. It angered Sang. He had not known peace since he arrived eight years ago. Sang viciously tore into Zi Han's throat, startling the woman at his side awake. Sang grabbed her by the neck mid scream as he held on to a feebly struggling Zi Han and crushed her windpipe with his claws that appeared without warning. He watched as the life faded from her face. Her mouth twisted with a scream that was cut short.

It was not long before someone sounded the alarm. He guessed he did not silence the woman fast enough, or they finally noticed he was no longer in his room. Sang released Zi Han's lifeless body before lightly touching it, again wishing it would go away. Once again, a bright green flame appeared and devoured not only Zi Han's body, but the woman's as well. He marveled at the flames that grew and spread when he heard the doors to the room slide open and a guard shout at him. Sang ran at the guard and forced him over the railing. He heard the crunch of bones, and the smell of copper filled his nose when they hit the stone path below.

Sang looked down to see the wide-eyed expression on the guard's contorted face. Panicked, he sprinted off the body as the other guards shouted after him. He climbed over the closest wall and ran as far as he could away from the compound. He stopped running briefly to turn and see that the main house had gone up in flames and that fire was spreading rapidly to the other buildings. The screams carried far and reached the ears of people from a great distance. Sang knew he had to escape from the grounds and leave China completely or they would hunt him for what he had done for however long his kind lived. So, he ran again.

He was bone weary, and the sun was rising. He had been running all night, and he did not know where he was now. The air smelled salty, and he could hear the crashing of water on land and the cry of birds. It had been a very long time since he smelled that kind of air or saw the sea. He could barely remember it. Though he was exhausted and hungry, he kept moving.

Sang had stumbled to his knees, landing on his hands in the sand. He had tried not to think about what had happened that night; he needed to focus on getting away, but the memories came flooding back and he purged himself of bile.

"Hey there! Are you well?" asked a stranger as he approached the vomiting boy.

Sang was not aware that someone was near him until they spoke. Frightened, he tried to back away, but he was in no condition to move much more or fight.

"It's all right, lad, I won't hurt you," he tried, extending a friendly hand.

"Billy? What's going on?" spoke another man.

"It's a kid. He looks scared shitless, though," replied Billy.

"I'd be scared shitless if I saw your mug, too," laughed the other man.

Sang watched the exchange, not sure of what either of the foreigners were saying. The sun had tanned their skin, and they had light hair. One was short and scruffy looking, and the other was tall and gangly.

"I don't think he speaks English, Billy," said the tall one.

"I can see that, Sam. I'm not stupid." Billy pulled something out of his pocket, a knife.

Sang's eyes went wide at the sight of the blade, and he backed away further. The one with the knife held his hands up in a mock surrender before pulling a small loaf of bread from his other pocket. He offered both to Sang. Sang cautiously moved over to the short, scruffy man and snatched the bread and knife from him. He quickly tore into the stale bread, all while holding the men at bay with the knife.

"You gave him a weapon? What for?" asked the bewildered tall man, Sam.

"So he'll trust me, ya idjit," said Billy.

"Is that so? What's to stop him from guttin' you with it?"

Billy scoffed. "He ain't in no shape to hurt a fly."

Sang continued to eat the bread and hold the knife up while they went back and forth. Once he had finished the bread, he held out his free hand.

"I think he wants more," said Sam.

"Yeah? Well, he's goin' to have to come with us for that. You see what he is, right?"

"I ain't seen one of them since I was a boy. Think he'll come with us on his own?"

"Dunno, but I aim to try," Billy said, smiling at the boy.

Sang saw the darkness in the short, scruffy one's eyes he did not like as he approached him. Sang brandished the knife more aggressively as he tried to get to his feet. The men only seemed to be amused. Sang tossed the rusted knife to the ground and stumbled to his feet to run, but he did not get far. The tall one got in front of him quickly and blocked his path. When Sang turned back around, the short one was now in front of him. The short one hit him hard across the jaw, sending Sang back to the ground. He tried to get back up, but the short one struck him in the face again. Before he blacked out, Sang felt someone with brawny arms lifting him up and carrying him away.

When Sang opened his eyes, he was no longer on the beach. He did not know where he was, but it moved in a way that made his stomach roll around and he was light-headed when he stood. He saw a small hole in the wall. When he peered through it, all he saw was water. He could feel the air flee from his lungs rapidly as he backed away from the hole. As he backed away, he grabbed onto a shelf, immediately setting it on fire. The smoke from the fire floated through the wood planks, and he could hear shouting followed by quick, heavy footfalls coming his way.

They threw buckets of water at him, and the fire, but the fire would not go out. The panicked men argued, but stopped when one of them pointed at Sang. Sang backed into the nearest wall and crouched down, trying to make himself as small as possible. A tall, lean man came over to him with a strange looking stick made of metal and wood, and he struck Sang in the head hard. Once again, he collapsed, and the world swirled into darkness.

Sang awoke to the feeling of his wrists burning and the sound of rattling chains. The fire was out, and things were calm once more, but he was in chains again. He escaped one prison just to wind up in another. His freedom was gone.

# CHAPTER 5

I vy and her crew had been out at sea for several more days before they had finally docked somewhere they could unload and sell their cargo. She walked around while her crew brought their ill-gotten goods ashore. There were few ships that day and the ones there were also unloading what they had, as well as resupplying. However, a crew unloading a junk ship had an interesting piece of cargo that they just tossed to the side and kept going with pulling more cargo off the ship.

She kept a safe distance from where they were dropping off crates and barrels, and she watched. She saw a man barking orders to the crew. He was of average height and build, with salt and pepper hair and a matching beard. Ivy assumed that he was the captain of the vessel. She waited until his men were not so close to him before making her approach.

"Excuse me, can I ask about a piece of cargo your men brought ashore?"

"Yeah, what is it?" he grumbled, not looking up to see who was talking to him. When he looked up, he grinned. "Oh! What would the lady like?"

Ivy returned his smile, but hid her fangs. She pointed to the Asian boy whom they had placed in irons just a few yards behind him. He was bleeding badly from the head and slumped over. "Where did you find him?"

The man turned his head slightly to see who she was referring to. "Him? We took him off a beach in China. He's been locked up in the hull for a while."

"How much do you want for him?" she asked.

"He's feral and don't speak. He nearly burned my ship to cinders," he started. "The boy's more trouble than he's worth."

Ivy smirked. "Sounds like a good deal to me. I'll take him off your hands if you like."

"He may be a lot of trouble, but he's also the last Andr to be seen in nearly two decades," he replied.

She tipped her hat to him. He knew what he had, and she was going to have to charm him into giving up the Andr or she would have to take him by force. "True enough. How much do you know about them?"

"Enough," he said, going back to giving orders and checking his list.

"Enough to know what happens if they're badly injured or starved?" she inquired.

"They can't die," he laughed.

"They can, and when they don't, you have a much bigger problem." She pointed at the Andr again.

They both watched as the Andr shifted, hearing bones crack and break as two pairs of large, black feathered wings shot out of his back in a bloody display, followed by a long, ax-bladed tail coming out of the base of his spine. The beast roared, his eyes glowing a vibrant white. The old, rusted chains they had him in broke apart and crumbled to the ground. Ivy concluded that the chains lacked iron or were too rusted to be effective. The beast took flight and dove back down onto an onlooker, too stunned to move. He tore into them and viciously ripped them to shreds before setting his sights on another person. The old man yelled to his men to capture the beast, but none would move.

"You know," Ivy laughed as the beast felled another person who was trying to take cover. "I can take care of that for you."

"You? A woman?" the old man scoffed.

Ivy smiled again. It was rare to find a soul that did not know who she was. She took out a dagger from inside her leather coat and threw it expertly into the heart of the beast. They both looked on as the beast fell out of the sky and to the ground. The moment he hit the sand, he exploded into a bright green blaze before turning into an ashen husk.

The old man took a few steps away from the strange women. This offered him a better look at her. Beneath a black tricorne hat was shoulder length, black tresses that just barely hid pointed ears. She had eyes as blue as the sea with a button nose and a pair of blood-red lips that showed a hint of fang. She wore men's clothes that fit her snuggly. Someone had to custom make them for her. She wore a tailored leather trench coat to conceal her slight frame. She was a beauty for sure, but she had to be a monster with the skill it took to take down an Andr in flight like she did.

Ivy smiled wickedly at him. "Now, what do you say? Can I have him?"

He narrowed his eyes at her. "What ship did you say you were with?"

"The Pale Emperor," she replied casually.

The old man cleared his throat nervously as he straightened himself out. "If he comes back, you can have him. He's far too much trouble," he replied sternly as he walked away.

Ivy called one of her men over and gave him the order to grab a set of iron chains and collect the Andr when he reformed.

Sang woke up naked on the ground, covered in his ashes. They immediately put him in chains again and placed a metal muzzle on his face. As they put him onto his feet, two new foreigners took Sang away to a large ship, leaving him confused and unable to comprehend what was happening. His wrists burned, but not his face. At least not as badly. Sang was tired and starving, but he had no hope that these foreigners would feed him anymore than the last ones had. He firmly believed that his destiny was to live a life as a slave, to be used and traded. He just wanted to be free. Whatever that meant.

# CHAPTER 6

S ang struggled at first, but the men escorting him aboard had a firm grip on him. These men smelled strange, powerful, and he was now even more concerned for his wellbeing. Once they got him aboard the ship, they took him to a dark hole in the floor with stairs that led downward. He struggled again as they took him below. He did not like being in the dark, even though he could see well enough. Bad things often happened in the dark.

They threw Sang into what looked like a cage and locked it. A small group of people gathered in front of the cage. He curled into himself and peered at them over his knees as they whispered and chatted amongst each other. He wished he could understand them. Desperately, he yearned to find out what fate awaited him. A petite woman dressed in men's clothing parted the growing crowd with ease and made her way to the front. She was absolutely captivating, and he stared. She had long, black curls that rested on her small shoulders and lips so red that they looked like they were bleeding. When she smiled, her pale skin lit up and he could see her fangs. He reached up to see if his were as long, but forgot about the muzzle on his face. The realization and the feel of defeat must have shown in his eyes because she frowned at him.

He watched as she summoned someone forward. The man was small and looked like him, in a way. He was bald and lean, with many scars on his arms and a few on his face. When the beautiful woman in men's clothing finished talking to him, the bald man approached the bars and beckoned Sang to him. Sang did not move. The man spoke to him in a language that sounded almost familiar, but Sang did not understand what was being said to him. The man speaking to him looked back at the woman before trying to speak to him again. This time Sang understood what he was saying.

Sang quickly got up and went to the front of the cage. His excitement and the speed with which he moved to grab the bars seemed to startle everyone. The man speaking to him told him to calm down when he babbled. Sang took a moment to collect himself, looking around at all the unfamiliar faces of men and women with amusement in their eyes, some with a touch of concern. He stepped away from the bars and sat back down on the floor, waiting to be asked another question. Once he had calmed down, the man, who introduced himself as Su Yang, the ship's doctor, asked who he was and how he got to this land.

Other than giving his name, Sang was at a loss at how he got there, but what was at the forefront of his mind was what was going to happen to him. He did not want to be chained up and kept in a cage. Su Yang relayed Sang's concerns to the woman. Sang watched as she took a few minutes to think about it and then gave her response to Su Yang. After giving her reply, she dispersed the crowd, much to their dismay, and then she left. Su Yang told Sang that he was being released from his chains and cleaned up, but that was all he told him.

Ivy waited anxiously in her cabin for Su Yang to bring the Andr to her. She looked over the food selections to make sure they met with her approval. There were slices of meat, various cheeses, and bread. It was not much, but she made sure her crew ate well. She had other means of obtaining nourishing sustenance. Being half succubus and half vampire made her a hypersexual dhampir, but she was not capable of draining a man's life force to the point of killing. At least not all at once. Her vampire nature gave her the ability to use magic, and it helped her hide her demonic half from those that hunted succubi and incubi. Her mother died protecting her from hunters and their order to kill them all. Despite her father's absence, she did not stay alone for long after her mother's death.

She shook her head to rid herself of the old memories. There was a guest to prepare for and she had to be at her best for when he arrived. As she wiped an errant tear from her eye, a knock came at her door.

"Excuse me, captain. I brought the young Andr as you requested. He has been cleaned up and made ready for you. Will there be anything else you need of me?" asked Su Yang.

He ushered a clean and nervous Sang into the room further.

Ivy watched the two men interact. The one called Sang was young, no more than eighteen or nineteen years old, maybe younger from the looks of him. The last one she saw died suddenly around fourteen years ago, but he never resurrected as he should have. He just turned to ash and blew away in the wind.

"Captain?"

"Hm? Oh, yes, please stay a moment if you have the time to spare. I know you still have injured to attend to," she replied.

"Yes, of course. My patients are stable for the time being. I can stay for a little while, but not too long."

"I understand. Can you ask him if he's hungry?"

Su Yang turned to the frightened boy and asked her question. Sang nodded vigorously and babbled quickly again. Ivy gestured towards the table with the meat, bread, and cheeses. She watched with amusement as the boy quickly made his way over and immediately started gorging himself. He had worked his way through a small part of the platter before he noticed he was being watched. Ivy smiled more when he offered her some.

"No, thank you. Please, eat your fill."

He looked at Su Yang for translation before finishing the entire table.

"My, he does have an appetite. Doesn't he?"

"Yes, Captain. It would appear that he has not had any food in some time." Su Yang gave Sang some ale to wash down all the food he had just consumed so greedily.

Ivy laughed when Sang half spit out the ale, scrunching up his nose to it. "Here, have some water instead," she said, handing him another cup. "He doesn't seem to like the taste of ale." She smiled again at how gingerly he took the water from her.

"No, it would appear not," Su Yang replied.

Ivy watched as Sang gulped down the water and wiped his mouth with the back of his hand. He was staring at her the whole time with his emerald green eyes. She walked over to him, and he immediately backed away, but Su Yang caught him and forced him to his knees. With one arm behind his back.

She grabbed his face and squeezed hard. "You're a pretty thing, aren't you?" she smiled suggestively. "And I do so love pretty things."

Sang shifted uncomfortably on his knees as he tried and failed to get out of her grasp. He did not understand what she had said, but she had the same look in her eyes that Leung had, and he did not like it.

Ivy released him, gently patting the side of his face. "You can let him go, Su."

"But captain, he is an Andr. What if he tries to hurt you?"

Ivy snorted with laughter. "Do you really think I can't handle an Andr?"

"No ma'am, but he is not Rae—"

She shot him a nasty look, cutting him off. "You can leave now," she growled.

"Captain…"

"I'll be fine," she said through gritted teeth.

Su Yang sighed and released Sang. He bowed his head, and then left the cabin, closing the door behind him.

Ivy took a moment to calm herself. She did not take kindly to being thought of as weak and incapable of taking care of herself. She also did not like being reminded of what she had lost. Looking down at the boy that was quivering in front of her, she smiled. Ivy had never known an Andr to be so frail and scared before. Though she was not that much older than him and she did not know many of their kind. She knew she had to be gentle with this one. He reminded her a lot of herself when she was younger than he was currently. What had made such a fearsome creature look so small and helpless?

Ivy gestured to her bed, but he did not move. Slowly and gently, she took him by the hand and led him over to it. He resisted at first, but she could be patient. So she waited before trying again. This time, he went along. She sat him down and stepped back a few feet. She watched him as he watched her with a mix of fear and curiosity. Keeping a gentle smile on her face, she disrobed. She continued to move slowly and made a show of revealing her body to him.

Once all of her clothes hit the floor, she moved closer to him. He had long, thin fingers with wide palms. His hands were warm against her bare breasts when she put them on her. She closed her eyes and moaned at the warmth sending jolts throughout her cold body. The sound must have frightened him because he tried to remove his hands, but she held him firm. The look on his face was one of confusion with a touch of concern. She wondered if he thought he was hurting her.

Careful not to scare him further, she let go of his hands and placed one of hers on his chest and pushed him back onto the bed so that he was laying down. This time, he did not resist her. She could see the tightness in his trousers and sought to relieve him of his growing tension. Her hand glided over the hardened mass purposefully, and when she freed him from the confines of the constricting material, her eyes lit up with surprise and excitement. She was not expecting him to have such length and girth. Oh, he was a prized find indeed!

When it sprang out of his trousers, Sang's erection stood tall and proud, causing his face to flush with embarrassment. Being so exposed made his breathing labored, but Ivy found him adorable. She did not bother speaking. He would not understand her, anyway. They would communicate through touch, and she was all too happy to teach him. She climbed on top of him, meeting his gaze. Lightly, she kissed him. It was a chaste kiss at first, her lips just barely brushing his, before she crushed hers to his with wanton passion. Her tongue urgently searched for entry into his mouth, but was denied.

She traipsed her fingers delicately along the underside of his cock before wrapping her fingers around it as much as she could. She stroked him slowly, making him gasp. Her tongue quickly made its way past his lips and made contact with his.

Their tongues played, and she felt the warm caress of his hands on her back. She could feel him relax as they kissed, enjoying the feel of his soft, warm skin. Soon his kiss deepened, and she could feel the hunger behind it. It occurred to her that this may be his first time, so she broke their fervent kiss. Again, he looked confused, but she wanted to take things slower, let him enjoy himself more. She smiled down at him and then gave him a light peck on the lips. There were so many wicked things that she wanted to do to him, but she needed to be patient with him. The sensations were probably foreign to him, and rushing things would do him a great disservice. No, she wanted him trained properly, and she needed him to want her.

Ivy made her way down his chest, lingering at his nipples for a moment, and gave them her full attention. She giggled when he hissed. Her saliva ran as cool as she did, and it always got that reaction from her more warm-blooded lovers. She continued her descent, leaving a cool trail behind until she reached her intended destination. Still in awe of his size, she marveled at how lovely it was to look at. She carefully smoothed down the foreskin to reveal the shining head. With the tip of her tongue, she lapped up the salty drop that leaked out. Again, he hissed, and she smiled as his hands firmly gripped the bedding. She hoped that the sensation felt good to him.

She dragged her wicked tongue up the underside of his manhood and then circled the head expertly. Working her jaw in preparation, she took him into her waiting mouth. She smiled when she heard him cry out. One of his hands found its way into her hair as she took more of him in. It had been quite some time since she had met with such a challenge, and she welcomed it with every intention of spoiling him. When she grabbed him by the balls, he arched up, momentarily gagging her, but she recovered quickly and took the entire length of him into her mouth.

With each loving stroke of her lips, accompanied by her tongue, she sucked him hard and fast until he could no longer hold back. He released his load down her throat, and she swallowed every bit until he had no more to give. She let him go, wiping her mouth of what did not make it down her greedy throat. He laid splayed out on her bed, his breaths even more labored as she watched him from where she kneeled. He appeared exhausted, but she had not finished with him. She intended to have her pleasures as well.

Ivy climbed back into her bed and observed that he was not as tired as she had assumed. He was still very erect, which pleased her. It was good that he had stamina; he was going to need it with her. She happily mounted her dragon and spread herself wide to accommodate his girth. Easing down on him slowly, it was her turn to hiss from the sensation. It had been far too long since she last took a lover; she was tight. Once she got as much of him in as she could handle, she looked down at him. His breathing had picked up again, but just slightly. She took hold of his hands and placed them on her hips, and then put her hands on his chest as she moved her hips back and forth slowly. A sigh slipped from her lips as she threw her head back, taking in more of him little by little.

As she rode him, moans reverberated through her, and she picked up speed. It did not take long for him to get a handle on things. Andr were always fast learners. His hands slid to her rear and gripped her firmly, forcing the rest of his cock into her. Her breath caught in her chest at the shock, be he did not seem to care as he ground her into him. She felt no pain; he was hitting all the right spots, and she bucked on top of him. Her erratic movements must have bothered him, because he grunted and growled before he flipped her on her back.

His thrusts came hard and fast as he grabbed her thighs, lifting them to get deeper into her. He was going to be an aggressive lover. So much for being gentle with him. All she could hear was the slapping of flesh against flesh and her cries of pure elation as he continued to grunt as he slammed into her with reckless abandon. She could tell he was close to his next release, she was close as well. Not to be a non-participant, she squeezed his cock as tightly as she could manage, considering how much he spread her open. The pressure she put around him made him come almost immediately, and with one final push, she came howling.

He released her legs and collapsed on top of her. This time, to make sure that he was done, she cradled him, and then bit into the side of his neck. She wrapped her legs around his waist and held him tight when he tried to get away. His ability to still move despite his exhaustion impressed her. She would have fucked him longer, but she was not quite ready for that. Ivy had plans for her dragon lover, and she needed him to understand what she wanted from him in and out of bed. For now, she would take her fill of his blood, and then let him rest. He most likely needed it more than he realized. His lessons would begin in the morning… if he was willing.

# CHAPTER 7

W hen Sang woke up, he was groggy and a little lightheaded. He vaguely recalled the previous night's activities, but he remembered it felt good, really good, until it did not. He rubbed his neck, but felt nothing. The bite wounds he remembered must have healed already. It was then that he realized he was alone. It was an odd feeling being on such a comfortable pallet. Though it was a lot different from what he was used to. There were soft furs and fluffy things with feathers in them he rested his head on. The pallet also stood higher off the ground, with wooden posts and legs. Perhaps it was not a pallet that he was lying on. Whatever it was, he really liked it.

Sang lingered in his comfort for a few moments longer before he decided he needed to get up. When his feet hit the floor, they landed on more warm fur. He let his feet play in the tufts of fur, smiling at the unfamiliar feeling. Once he had his fill of the soft fur, he moved towards the door. To his surprise, he found it was not locked. He stepped out, shielding his eyes from the harsh morning light. Walking out onto the deck, he froze. Panicked, he sprinted to the railing that surrounded the large vessel and peered over the side. He quickly made his way over to the other side, only to see the same thing. Water. No land in sight. Sang backed away in shock, clutching his chest as if trying to prevent his heart from jumping out. The sounds of laughter seemed far away as he fell to his knees, hyperventilating. A gentle hand touched his shoulder, and Sang nearly jumped out of his skin. Su Yang did his best to calm Sang, but the lack of air eventually made him pass out.

When Sang regained consciousness, unfamiliar faces again surrounded him. Some of them looked concerned. He tried to sit up, but immediately regretted doing so.

The motion of the vessel made his stomach uneasy, and he emptied the contents of it onto the deck. Su Yan gently patted his back until he was done. He heard groaning and assumed it was because of the mess he had just made. The group dispersed, leaving him with Su Yang. Once he was done, he wiped his mouth with a shaky hand and looked up at Su Yang. Su Yang had a sympathetic look on his weathered face. The first thing Sang asked was where they were going. To which Su Yan replied with nowhere. He took a moment to answer, as if he was not sure that Sang would be all right with the alternative, but Sang did not care where they were going so long as it was not to China.

"Is he all right?" came a familiar voice.

Sang turned to confirm that it was the woman from yesterday. He scrunched up into himself, wrapping his arms around his knees as he watched her and Su Yang talk. Su Yang turned to him and told him what the woman, Ivy, had said. She wanted to know how he was feeling after last night. Sang was unsure of how to answer. He did not know exactly what they were doing, but he did not like being bit. His freedom was important to him, and he did not like being in chains and held captive.

Su Yan relayed what he said to Ivy. She laughed at first, and when Su Yang continued, she frowned. Sang wondered what part of what he said made her frown.

Ivy sighed. "Very well. Tell him he is free to go when we get close to the nearest settlement, but he needs to know that he won't be safe on his own. He's weak and can't take care of himself, especially if he doesn't understand or speak English," she started, folding her arms over her chest. "If he stays, I can make sure he's safe, warm, and fed. We can train him to fight and protect himself. He'll never be in chains again or bought and sold, but it has to be his decision."

"Are you sure about this, captain? What if Tempest finds out about him? Again, he is not—"

"I know," she snapped, cutting him off again. "Just tell him what I said and say nothing else."

Sang caught the warning in her tone. Su Yang had said something that upset her again.

"Aye, captain," he replied.

Su Yang turned back to Sang and took a deep breath before relaying Ivy's words. She was giving him a choice. He was not sure what to do with that. On the one hand, he would be free and on his own, but she was right. He did not know enough about the outside world to take care of himself properly. With what he was, he would likely be caught and put back in chains. He did not want that, and though it would probably be for his own good, he was not sure that learning to fight was right for him. He did not like violence. Staying aboard this ship was likely the best course of action, but at what cost?

"He wants to know if he stays will he have to share a room and pallet with you?"

"A pallet? Does he mean a bed?" she laughed.

"I believe so," Su Yang smiled.

Sang wondered what he said that was so amusing to them.

"He also wants to know if you will steal more of his blood?"

The Ivy woman's eyes went wide briefly, and she paused to think something over. Sang wished he knew what was actually being said. As if sensing his concern, Su Yang patted his head to reassure him he was telling her everything that he wanted to know. At least he hoped that was what he was trying to convey to him.

"Tell him yes, his blood and body will serve as payment for his food and boarding." He is welcome to bunk with the others if he isn't in the mood to fuck. And he is welcome to my blood if he feels so inclined to take it."

Whatever she said suddenly had Su Yang worried, but before he could express his concerns, she held up her small hand to stop him.

"If he stays, he will need to learn to speak English, I insist."

"Yes, captain," Su Yang replied, then told Sang what she had said.

Sang was not sure how he felt being used for his body and his blood, but he understood that his limited freedom would come at a price. He did like that he would not be put in chains or sold to someone else, and the option to room with the others was a plus. Though he was not familiar with anyone other than Su Yang and Ivy. He decided he would stay with this group until he could fend for himself.

Ivy nodded when Su Yang told her what he had said. "Good. Tell him his training will start when my Valravn return." With that, she turned and left.

Sang watched her walk away with her arms wrapped around herself. He suddenly felt sad for her. Even though so many others surrounded her, she still appeared to be lonely.

Ivy walked up to the ship's wheel and took over steering. A tall man followed her shortly after.

"Yes, what is it, Dutch?" she asked, not bothering to look over at him.

"What's on your mind, captain?"

"Nothing, I'm fine. Now go away."

"As your quartermaster, I would believe that and follow orders. But as your friend, I call bullshit," he said with a smirk.

She turned and glared at the man. "I hate how observant you are," she grumbled.

"I know you do, but you know it's for the best. Otherwise, you wouldn't have much use for me."

"Yes, you are pretty old," she laughed.

"True enough, so let this old man impart some wisdom onto you," he retorted, his hands behind his back and a stern look on his scruffy face.

"Fine, let's have it then," she sighed.

"I see you're worried that you'll lose another dragon, but you have to keep in mind that he's not—"

"Don't. Don't say his name... please," she interrupted.

"He's not him. This one is fragile, and your attempts to seduce and control him will not work."

"It certainly seems that way," she said solemnly, focusing her attention on keeping the ship on course and listening to her first mate.

"Did you see that brand on the back of his neck?" he asked curiously.

"I did."

"That's a slave brand. Perhaps a softer touch and more patience would work better than fucking him into a stupor?"

"Can't blame me for trying," she said with a smirk. "It's in my nature, after all."

"I am acutely aware of your nature. We all are. We heard everything last night."

She blushed. "Sorry, it's been a while for me."

"Not that long, Ivy," he said, narrowing his eyes at her.

"For me, it has been."

"Either way, he's fresh and ignorant of your nature."

"Not after last night, he isn't," she laughed again.

"Mind me, girl. You're not so old that I won't bend you over my knee," he fussed.

She went quiet.

"You and he aren't so different. You were both beholden to the whims and desires of others. Maybe keep that in mind the next time you try to bed him."

"Aye, aye, captain." She gave him a mock salute.

"Mock me all you want, but if you don't want to lose him, then consider what he might have been through. You are not Alexander Tempest."

The smile left her face at his words. He was right. She had to do some things differently to keep her dragon.

The last port had little in the way of entertainment, so the Pale Emperor moved on to the next, after trading off the goods they stole with the help of mermaids. Her crew was still feeling restless, and very much in need of a good drink with the company of whores to spend their new fortune. Maybe a game or two. Ivy was familiar with the port town they were in, as was most of her crew. Those not on duty took to the local public houses. Many of them would be broke by the night's end, so Ivy needed to have a new score lined up.

With Sang and a few others in tow, Ivy made her way to a brothel with a tavern. Prostitutes looking for a quick and easy coin immediately took the men in her group away. She had nothing against prostitutes, her mother was one, so she understood them. She warned them away from Sang and a human boy with her.

"Ivy Thatch? Is that you, girl?" came a familiar voice.

Ivy smiled as she turned towards the older woman. "Hello, Mary."

"It's been far too long since I've seen that beautiful face of yours!" said Mary, an old woman barely holding onto the blonde in her hair. "How've you been? I hear you're a ship's captain now."

"Yes," Ivy said, trying not to be smothered by the other woman's ample and over perfumed bosom.

"About time that rat bastard saw you for bein' more than your mother's daughter. Kept you safe, though, didn't he?"

Safe was not the word she would have used for how Alexander Tempest kept her. "Sure," she decided.

Mary stepped back a bit to get a better look at Ivy. "You look good, but I suppose that's to be expected considerin' your blood."

Mary always made a compliment insulting. Ivy was glad to be free of the old madam. She wished her mother had rid herself of the horrid woman sooner. Perhaps she would still be alive. Life as a whore's daughter was no real life and she would have ended up a whore as well, but at least there was the chance that she would have never met Tempest. Despite how awful the demon was, she would not trade her life as it was for anything. She was as free as a half-bred succubus could be. So long as she kept that part of her hidden. Ivy hated denying her mother's blood, but her continued survival depended on it.

"Looks like you could use a stiff drink," said Mary, interrupting Ivy's thoughts.

"Yeah, that'd be nice. Thanks," Ivy replied.

"So, what have you been up to all these years? Any good scores?" she asked as she led the trio to the bar.

Ivy smirked. It was just like an old whore to try to pry information from a patron. Old habits died hard, if at all. "A few here and there," she said, taking a seat.

"I know ale for you, but what about the young pups trailin' behind you?"

"That one," she started, pointing at Sang, "Doesn't drink."

"Funny lookin' lad, ain't he? What about the other one?"

"Tommy? He's a big boy and can order for himself," Ivy replied. "He's human, though, so be nice to him."

"When am I ever not nice?"

She feigned offense, handing Ivy her tankard of ale and a glass of water to Sang.

"All right, love, what'll it be?" she asked Tommy.

"I'll have a beer," he replied.

"If you lot need anythin' else, just let Sadie know. You remember Sadie, don't you?"

Ivy nodded as she drank.

"All right, then. I've got a house to run. We'll catch up more later," she said, sauntering off.

Good riddance, Ivy thought as she continued to drink.

Ivy sat in silence for a while with Sang quietly observing her and the room. Tommy sat close by, nursing his drink. Ivy pricked her ears to listen out for anything interesting. After about an hour of eavesdropping on various conversations, she found her target. A merchant sailor, drunk off his ass, was going on about cargo that he was supposed to keep secret to the girl who sat in his lap. She was a plain-looking girl. Ivy would have no trouble taking the chatty sailor away from her.

"Hey, Tommy, keep an eye on Sang. I'll be back in a couple of hours," she ordered, pushing off the bar stool.

Tommy grabbed Sang while downing the last of his beer before the boy could follow Ivy. He sat him back down with little effort.

Ivy casually walked over to the engaged pair and bumped the poor girl out of the sailor's lap and onto the floor. When the girl got up to protest, Ivy smiled, baring her fangs and a look that dared her to try anything to remove her. The sailor laughed drunkenly at the exchange. The girl stormed off in a huff. Ivy thought she was doing the girl a favor. The sailor was not the best looking and smelled bad. It was all Ivy could do not to retch in front of him.

"So, what's a looker like you doin' in my lap?" he asked, slurring his words.

Good, he was almost completely hammered. Getting what she needed from him would be easy, so long as he did not pass out on her. Or under her, for that matter.

"You looked bored. I thought a handsome sailor deserved a girl that could show him a real good time," she purred in his ear, swallowing the bile that surged at the back of her throat. This would not be as easy as she initially thought. That girl was clearly human and had a poor sense of smell.

"Oh really? What's it gonna cost me?"

So, he was not as drunk as she thought, either. "Keep your coin. I'm just looking for a bit of fun. You up for it?"

"With you? Absolutely!"

"Good," she smiled devilishly. She got up, breathing in as much air clear of his stench as she could before she would be locked in a room with him. "Sadie," she called across the room as she led the man towards the stairs near the bar.

"Four's open for ya," shouted a large woman from across the room without looking back.

"Come on, sailor. Your dreams await upstairs."

The merchant sailor happily stumbled up the stairs behind her. Ivy hoped the secret cargo was worth what she was about to do.

Sang watched as Ivy took a man upstairs. He did not know what would happen to the man or to Ivy, but this was his chance to get away.

"Don't even think about it," said Tommy, drawing his pistol as he continued to drink.

Sang smelled the black powder on the weapon and recognized it as being a smaller version of one of the other ones that he had been hit with. He adjusted himself on the stool and settled into continue watching the room in silence. He was not going anywhere until Ivy returned.

Sang watched as people milled about, intoxicated and having a good time. Multiple females and a few males had taken notice of him. He assumed that some of them thought he was for sale and the others stared at him like he was an oddity. He supposed he was, since he was the only one in the room that looked like him. In a room full of thieves, he was nervous. Especially when his scales looked like valuable gems. He wore long sleeves and trousers, though they were too hot for his liking and ill-fitting, to hide the scales on his shoulders, sides, and abdomen. His hair was long enough to cover the scales near his hairline and the feathers at the nape of his neck. Still, he was different, and even the drunks could tell.

After some time had passed, Ivy returned downstairs. She quickly made her way down the stairs and looked as if she was going to empty the contents of her stomach at any moment. She made her way over to him, and a now passed out Tommy, who moaned in his sleep, and snatched them both up.

"We're leaving," she said, then bolted for the door.

Sang was not sure of what she had said, but from the looks of her, they needed to leave. He looked up at the stairs, not sure of what he was expecting, but nothing happened, and no one followed her down. He was curious to know what made her so sick.

Once the sun rose, the stragglers of the crew that had been out too late had staggered back to the ship. They cast off and left the port. Whatever happened upstairs in that tavern, Ivy was not willing to speak about it. She barked orders at the hungover helmsman, and they were on their way.

# CHAPTER 8

I t was well into the evening when someone spotted them flying in. Kuasa and Kamau. The Valravn. They had landed on the main deck, where Ivy was waiting for them. Their landing was both graceful and shocking, as they seamlessly transformed from their large avian forms to human ones. Ivy thought they were both sights to behold. They were twins with golden brown eyes and dark brown skin. Kuasa was tall and lithe. Her hair was a crown of long, black locs she kept in multiple braids that ended just below her breasts. She used a thin, red string to wrap the braids. She had a beauty mark near her right eye, just as Sang did. It made Ivy a little jealous. Kuasa had a cute little nose that sat above a pair of full, light-colored lips. She had a long, elegant neck that she adorned with beads and colored ropes of varying lengths.

Kamau, Kuasa's twin brother, was as handsome as he was joyful. His hair was as long as his sister's and he kept it in braided locs as well. He braided his locs in neat rows, going to the back of his head with the sides shaved close. Kamau wrapped the ends of his locs in a thin, red string and wrapped thin strips of metal around a few locs in various places along the braids. He had a small scar in the center of his left eyebrow. His nose was arrow shaped and sat above a full pair of lips that matched his skin. Small hoops in his ears held dangling pointed pendulums, and he adorned his thick neck with colored ropes and a string of metal points. Where Kuasa was tall and athletic, Kamau was tall and barrel-chested.

It was clear in the way Kuasa carried herself that she was a strong and proud woman. She was the more serious of the two, and Kamau often got under her skin with how playful he was. Their mother, a Valravn, was a Brazilian slave from Liberia. Their father, a shapeshifter, was her master. He did not acknowledge his children, and they ignored their shifter blood. Choosing only to transform into Valravn. They were both well-trained fighters that, like their mother, spent part of their lives grounded. The slavers did not allow them the chance to spread their wings. If anyone tried, the slavers would shoot them out of the sky.

Ivy had killed their father and many of his men during a raid, freeing all slaves. As thanks for setting them all free, the twins agreed to serve as Ivy's familiars. Ivy did not take kindly to slavers and had no interest in being one herself. As her familiars, she still paid them a wage for the work they did for her. Ivy included them as part of her crew and family, allowing them to come and go as they pleased.

Ivy hugged both of them, followed by a kiss on their cheeks. She lightly punched Kamau in the arm for blushing, which made him smile and blush more.

"Good evening, captain," started Kuasa. "We got back as soon as we could, but someone," she elbowed her brother in the side, "saw another pretty girl."

"Really, Kam?" Ivy laughed.

"I could not help myself, captain. She was a true beauty," he replied, smiling brightly.

"They always are with you. Now, did you bring me anything good?"

"Not this time, but the King of Tides requests an audience," said Kuasa.

Ivy understood the look in Kuasa's eyes. The King of Tides, Alexander Tempest, never called the Pale Emperor back unless it was for an important job. Though she did not understand why he did not just tell the twins what he wanted rather than summon her.

Ivy sighed. "All right, we'll head that way soon. First, I have someone I want you two to meet." She motioned for Sang and Su Yang to come over.

Sang was nervous about meeting someone new. He was still adjusting to the surrounding crew. Many of them had dark skin, at least darker than his, but not like the two that he was being presented to. They had skin the color of the night sky and brilliant white teeth when they smiled. Su Yang had told him they were Valravn, great, large birds; and that, like him, they were slaves once. He was told that their names were Kuasa and Kamau, and they were from Brazil. The female night skin stared at him in wonder and amazement as she walked around inspecting him.

"Are you sure that he is an Andr? He is so small, and he looks weak," spoke the one called Kuasa, turning up her lip in dissatisfaction. "How are we supposed to teach this," she gestured to all of him, "to fight?"

The male night skin, Kamau, grinned at him. "Come now, sister. He might surprise you."

Sang wished even harder that he could speak English, or, at the very least, understand it. He had the feeling that he was being looked down on. He turned to Su Yang for translation, and Su Yang responded with a forced smile, telling him it was not important. Now he was certain that he received an insult.

"And does not speak English?" Kuasa threw up her hands and walked away.

Kamau followed her in laughter.

"The look of ire must have shown on his face because Kamau turned Kuasa towards him and she sighed, softening her expression.

"Fine. How would you like us to train your dragon?"

"Excellent! I appreciate this more than you know," said Ivy. "You will, of course, be well compensated for your time and skills."

"There is no need for that, Captain." I am uncertain if we can teach him at all.

"Careful, sister. I think you have hurt his feelings."

"If he is an Andr, then he has none to hurt," she spat.

"You are still upset that the last one bested you," Kamau laughed.

Kuasa pointed a stern finger at her brother. "That fight was a draw! He did not beat me."

Sang continued to watch the exchange with a mix of confusion and irritation. Su Yang was of no help as he had walked away. Before Sang could express his frustration, Ivy spoke again. She said something to the two night skins, and they bowed at the waist to her before walking away. Su Yang was called back over, and told him that his training would begin when they made landfall some place close that was uninhabited. They asked him where he wanted to sleep, and he quickly decided to share a bed with Ivy, but only for sleeping. She nodded her agreement and led him back to her cabin.

Morning had come, and they soon reached the beach of what appeared to be a deserted island. It was late in the morning when they got off the ship. They went as far back on the beach as they could before hitting a line of trees. There, Kuasa and Kamau made a space to train Sang. First, they sparred with each other, just so Sang could see what he would need to be doing.

Sang watched them closely as they moved. Their movements were fluid and rhythmic as they swung their bodies side to side, each going in the opposite direction of the other. It looked as if they were dancing in a way. Their dancing soon turned into rhythmic flips and low cartwheels as they moved around each other. When one swept their leg, the other would hop over it. They continued in this way briefly before making contact. Each strike was purposeful and powerful. Kuasa crouched down low onto one hand, and then quickly brought her leg up to strike Kamau and he barely had time to block his side before she hit him. The kick sent him sliding sideways in the sand and he skidded to a halt, still holding his arms up in defense. He cursed under his breath before going back into his rhythmic swing. Kuasa did the same.

Their sparring went on for longer, Sang watching them intently, completely transfixed, before they stopped all together. Su Yang urged Sang towards the pair when Kuasa motioned for him to come over. Sang was naturally nervous, but Kamau had that bright, friendly smile of his that put Sang a little more at ease. Kuasa gently tapped his shoulder to get his attention. She wanted to show him the basic movements. Su Yang translated what she said so that Sang would have a better understanding of what she wanted from him.

Sang nodded. He was ready for Kamau. At least he
hoped he was. He did his best to mimic the movements
Kuasa showed him, but he knew it was sloppy. He
honestly had no sense of rhythm, but he was at least going
to try. Kamau kept swinging from side to side for a while,
and Sang followed suit. Suddenly, Kamau moved in on
him and looked as if he was going to strike Sang with his
hand, but he twisted his upper body down behind him
onto his hands, and then both his feet came up rapidly and
hit Sang in the head, sending him just as quickly to the
ground. Sang hit his head hard when he landed on his
back. He immediately put his hand to the back of his head
and drew blood.

Su Yang quickly made his way over, but Ivy had called
to him.

"Pick him up. He can keep going," she ordered.

"But captain, he is bleeding badly from the head," Su
Yang contested.

"He's an Andr. He'll heal," she countered.

Su Yang got Sang back on his feet. Sang wanted to stop.
He felt a slight pressure in his head, and he was dizzy. Su
Yang relayed what Ivy had said as he dabbed at the wound
with a cloth. He assured Sang that he would be all right
and that he could keep going if he did not think about the

injury. Sang nodded his agreement, instantly regretting
doing so. He stumbled a bit, but Su Yang caught him.

Again, Sang tried to mimic the swinging movements,
but it was sluggish and even more sloppy. Kuasa had
shouted at him, but she might as well have been under
water because he did not understand and could barely
hear her. Kamau had a worried look on his face as he
swung side to side, most likely waiting for Sang to heal
and be ready, but he collapsed to the ground instead. The
force from Kamau's kick and how hard he landed had him
feeling nauseous and weak now. In an instant, he felt a
surge of heat, and he was aware of what would occur
next. He let the darkness take him. He was tired, and no
longer wanted to fight.

"Shit," Ivy swore. She pulled a dagger from her coat, as
she had done before. "Move!"

Kuasa and Kamau both backed away at Ivy's order.
Sang's wings and tail had formed from his scales and back
in their bloody display. Once he was airborne, Ivy threw
her dagger, but missed. It was as if he was ready for her
this time. He was learning in his berserker state. He
swooped down to grab the closest person below him, but
Ivy pushed the seaman out of the way and Sang got her
instead. She fought him in the air as she pulled another
dagger out. She cut his hand and made him drop her. Ivy

fell to the ground and landed in a crouched position on one hand. Once she had good enough balance, she turned in time to see Sang barreling towards her. She rolled out of the way, throwing sand in his eyes as she did so. Still holding the dagger and now on her back, she threw the blade straight into his heart while he wiped the sand from his eyes.

Sang fell dead to the ground in a burst of bright green flames, leaving an ashen husk behind. Kuasa and Kamau ran to her side, picking her up. Not only did they serve as her familiars, but they also served as bodyguards. When she was on her feet again, she dusted herself off. They all watched as the husk broke apart and Sang came out of it.

"Get him something to wear," Ivy ordered at no one in particular.

The crewman she saved ran back to the ship to retrieve clothes.

"See, I told you he was not worth training," said Kuasa.

"He'll be fine. He just needs some more practice," Ivy countered.

"Maybe I should go a little easier on him," said Kamau. "I hit him pretty hard."

"Hit him hard. It'll toughen him up faster." Ivy did not even look at the twins when she spoke. She directed her focus towards Sang.

Kuasa noticed that. "He is not Rae—"

Ivy gave her a nasty, warning look before she could finish the name. "Just get him trained," she ordered as she walked away. "And give no quarter."

Kamau grinned. "Well, at least we can see why she likes him so much," he snickered, staring at an exposed Sang.

Kuasa punched him in the chest for the comment and then walked away.

The training went on well into the evening. Sang was showing improvement each time he reformed. He had died a few more times before he got the hang of the movements and found his sense of rhythm. However, he still got injured, and the wounds were not healing well. He boarded the ship and went to see Su Yang straight away.

Su Yang was finishing up with a crew member Sang had injured when he was in his berserker state. The girl quickly skittered by him as if he would attack her again. Had it not been for Ivy, Kuasa and Kamau acting as fast as they had, he probably would have done more than injure people. Su Yang had told him he was far more intelligent in his berserker rage than any Andr that he had come across. Sang did not know if he should be concerned about that or not. He felt bad about it, though.

His current concerns were his fresh wounds and exhausted muscles. Who knew what he considered dance fighting would be so dangerous? Su Yang advised him to be more respectful of the art and to not let the twins hear him call it that. It was an important part of who they were. Sang noted the warning. He noticed that Su Yang wore strange wrist bands that held many small, sharp needles. He would pull some out and stick them in what Sang thought were random places around his wounds, but they were not random at all. Su Yang made use of what he called acupuncture techniques to aid in his healing skills. Whatever that was, it took the pain away, and it fascinated Sang.

Su Yang was the only one on the ship outside of Ivy and the night skins that were not terrified of him. He was also told to never refer to the twins as night skins, especially in front of them. They carried weapons and Kuasa had a bad temper. They did not use weapons during his training outside of a long stick, but Sang noticed Kuasa's temper. She would strike him repeatedly in the same spot until he learned to defend it. Each strike was harder than the last, and he felt bones break, eventually. He was told that she caved in his skull with that same stick when he went into his berserker rage. There was some malice behind it, he was sure of it. She did not seem to like him very much.

As he pinned and stitched up the more severe wounds, Su Yang told him about Andr and their unique abilities. Aside from healing quickly, Andr had saliva that could heal most outer wounds and make it look like it was never there. Andr could spit acid, which was why they put him in a muzzle when they found him. Another disturbing ability of the Andr was their venomous bite, but if they knew sufficient control, it would paralyze instead of kill. Fire wielding was their most notable ability. Unfortunately, the blood of others was required to cultivate it. At least certain minerals in the blood, anyway.

Sang found the information about his kind extremely interesting. The good doctor also made it a point to teach him English at the same time. Sang wanted to know more, but that was all that Su Yang knew before they all disappeared, seemingly all at once. He was the last that anyone had seen in fourteen years, Sang's actual age. Andr hatched, looking to be at the age of four and aged normally from there until adulthood. Su Yang had said that he encountered different types of Andr when he was younger. He counted at least three types: forest, desert, and mainland. Sang was a mainland type, which meant he was more human than the other two feral types.

Once Su Yang finished stitching up Sang's wounds, Sang asked him if he would teach him how to use the needles while he helped him with his English. Su Yang said he needed to run the idea by Ivy first, but Sang pleaded for him not to do that. He did not think she would approve of him learning the skill because it did not have combat applications, and she seemed all too keen on him learning to fight. Sang did not enjoy fighting and wanted to learn a skill that could help others. Su Yang denied him once more and then sent him off to bed. He told him that acupuncture was dangerous if not done correctly, and Andr were natural warriors.

Though he was reluctant to do so, he left Su Yang to clean his tools and close his station for the night. He too had a long day and needed rest. So, Sang made his way back to the captain's quarters and back to the ever insatiable Ivy Thatch. Despite not wanting to go to her bed, he did not want to be in the same area as Kuasa either, and he found he had some pent-up frustration and energy he needed to expel before he could sleep. He would indulge her lust this night.

# CHAPTER 9

Ivy watched as he slept, marveling at his scales and the soft, downy feathers at the nape of his neck. He was feeling amorous last night; it surprised her. She was quite happy to oblige him, as she was in a lustful mood as well. Though his communication skills were nearly nonexistent, he was an apt student and very attentive. He understood almost perfectly what she wanted him to do, and she reciprocated his attention with all the skills she had been trained with. After hours of doting on one another, she finally got him to fall asleep.

He was definitely going to run circles around her when it came to stamina.

She lightly ran her fingers around the square-shaped scar near the base of his skull, just above his first armored spinal plate. It had Chinese lettering on it, a house symbol. It looked burned into him, but fire had no effect on Andr. The only way it could have gotten there was if someone used an iron branding tool that was struck by lightning. That would explain why it never went away after his many deaths. Wounds made of iron never healed and were the only way to leave behind scars on an Andr. They typically had thick hides, and one would have to be strong and skilled to injure one without an iron weapon. Kuasa and Kamau had a lot of practice with that before...

Her touching the old scar must have bothered him because he stirred, turning on his back, revealing the strange-looking mark on his chest over his heart. It was not a brand like the one on his neck. No, it looked like... was it a birthmark? Her curiosity got the better of her, and she could not help but touch it. Touch him. His sleep turned fitful as she traced the dragon in a figure-eight pattern that looked as if it was trying to catch its tail. That looked fitting for him, but it also had a flame with a crown wrapped around it that was centered on top of the segmented dragon.

She wondered what haunted him so badly that he could not find peace in his sleep. As a dhampir, she could use magic. And the stronger the blood she consumed, the more powerful she was. She had fed on him recently and felt strong enough to summon a storm, but for him she would use the power he gave her to bring him the peace that he needed. With a gentle caress of her hand over his heart, she could ease the pain he seemed to be in. Slowly, his breathing regulated, and he cried out less and less until he finally stilled.

When he opened his eyes, Ivy's worried face greeted him. It was then that he realized her eyes were two different shades of blue. The right one was noticeably darker than the left, the color of a stormy sky over the sea. His hand covered the hand that was resting lightly over his heart before it was withdrawn. He found the reaction to his touch confusing, considering how she normally insisted on being in contact with him. As he sat up, she moved away and covered herself with the fur blanket, blushing as she did so. He gave her a curious look in response.

Ivy felt ridiculous for her sudden bashfulness, but using her magic on him without his consent was wrong. Even if it was for his benefit. She looked up to see that he was staring at her with a look of confusion in his eyes. Again, she blushed and pointed to the mark on his chest. She watched as he examined the mark before opening his mouth to explain. He seemed to get flustered in his attempt to speak, and then angry when he could not find the words. She gently placed her hand back on his chest and used her magic to calm him again.

It surprised her when, instead of calming down, his pupils fully dilated, and he moved faster than she thought him capable of. Before she could react, he had her pinned beneath him with her hands in his above her head. His free hand was firmly around her throat. Had it been someone other than him, she would have taken it as a threat, but his sudden aggression gave her a rush, and she found herself wanting. Her bare breasts rose and fell rapidly with the surge of adrenaline.

There was something feral in the way he growled into her neck, his fangs lightly grazing her throat, followed by his tongue. She could feel his erection rubbing against her as he pressed his hips down. She could not decide what she felt more of—fear or curiosity. A feral Andr was dangerous to be sure, and she froze when he bit down on her neck. It was not a vicious bite. No blood was drawn, and no venom released, but it did nothing to relieve her increase in fear. When she struggled, his free hand stilled her movements with a force of strength that was both strong and a polite warning not to move again.

Ivy obeyed the silent order as he met her gaze. There was definitely a hint of something more within him, but she did not know if it was friend or foe. She continued to watch almost helplessly as his eyes moved down her body. It was as if he was deciding what he wanted to do. She could have gotten out from under him, but her inquisitive side had gotten the better of her again. He let her hands go in that moment, using that hand to hold his weight above her. His free hand found her breast, quickly followed by his tongue. The way his tongue wrapped around her nipple before the warmth of his mouth descended on it, coaxed an audible 'oh' from her she did not recognize as her own voice.

She could feel his fangs lightly scrape against her supple flesh as he pulled more of her breast into his mouth, causing her to arch into him. There was a rumble of another growl that reverberated through her, as if he disapproved of the movement. She dared to look down when he moved to the other breast. An animalistic luster covered his emerald green eyes that were staring menacingly back at her, daring her to move without his permission again. Part of her wanted to disobey him, just to see what he would do to her, but she knew better than to piss off a dragon. Even if he was on the scrawny side. It helped that his fangs were close to breaking skin.

He traveled down her body at an agonizingly slow pace. It was all she could do not to move him along faster, but she did not want to upset him. It was as if he could sense her growing frustration; he was suddenly smiling up at her when the tip of his tongue stabbed at her navel. A few painfully slow moments later, she could feel the warmth of his breath at her core. He nuzzled her lightly covered mound, inhaling her scent. She cried out when the flat of his tongue ran along her slit; the tip flicking her little bud before his lips caught it. He gently bit it, sending jolts of electricity throughout her body.

He groaned out, "Wèi wǒ gēchàng, wǒ kě'ài de xiǎoniǎo."

She did not know what he had said to her, but it sounded so good at that moment. His hands found their way to the underside of her thighs and pushed them farther apart, exposing her to the cresting morning light from her window. It surprised her when he wrapped his mouth around her lower lips and slid his tongue inside. Almost expertly, he tongued and sucked her core. He murmured the same words as she cried out even more, his tongue dancing inside of her, tirelessly working until she completely surrendered under his oral assault. He held her in a firm grip as she shuddered and bucked with an overwhelming wave of passion, giving him all that she had to offer, all that he had earned, into his waiting mouth. It left her wondering when exactly he learned to do that. Whatever was done to cause this sudden shift within him, she enjoyed it most thoroughly.

Once she came down from her high, he had moved to a kneeling position between her legs, one hand at her hip and the other on his pulsing cock. She was not ready for whatever he was going to do next, but that did not seem to matter to him. He grinned malevolently at her as he pulled her to him, placing the head of his manhood at her still quivering entrance. Still smiling, he leaned down until he was a breath away from her, and then slid himself into her too hard and too fast. Before she could get the scream that caught in her throat out, his mouth had captured hers in a fierce kiss. Now both of his hands were on her hips, establishing a harsh staccato rhythm.

He buried his face in the side of her neck, locking his teeth around her flesh. She wrapped her arms and legs around him while he fucked her until she moaned with pleasure again. Was he marking her? Ivy wanted to bite down on his should, but he was behaving erratically, and she did not want to challenge him. Instead, she enjoyed the feeling of him filling her so completely that she thought she might burst.

She whimpered when he stopped abruptly and pulled out, but he was not done with her. He flipped her over, getting a surprised yelp from her, and raised her rear so he could enter her from behind. His cock hit different from that angle. She buried her face into the pillow, but she could not contain her pleasure. She threw her head back and unleashed a powerful cry that she knew could be heard throughout the ship. And she did not care.

It felt like days had passed before he finally grunted his release into her and let her go. She knew she was limber, but he twisted and manipulated her body in ways she did not believe possible. When he was done with her, she was so completely spent that she passed out where and how he had left her.

Quietly, he crept out of Ivy's cabin, careful not to wake her. He vaguely remembered what happened between them, and his whole body ached with what he could make out from the fog of his mind. The sun was barely in the sky, but he needed to see the doctor. Perhaps Su Yang would have a salve to help his tired muscles.

Only a skeleton crew moved around when Sang left Ivy's quarters that morning. With some luck, it was not too early to visit Su Yang. Not only did he have complaints about his sore muscles, Sang's head felt strange, as if something had come loose within his mind. It did not feel right to him. He also wanted to ask him to teach him acupuncture again. Sang was determined to learn a useful skill that did not involve hurting others for when he was strong enough and knew enough about the world to strike out on his own. He did not want to be a burden or a slave anymore. He knew he would also need to master, or at least better control his own abilities.

He got to Su Yang's quarters without being seen. He hoped he reached Su Yang's quarters without being seen. Sang did not know why he felt the need to sneak around. He had been told that he was free to move about if he wanted, so long as he did not get in anyone's way. Still, he had learned to avoid being seen or heard, and unlearning those lessons right away was difficult. Before he could knock, Su Yang had opened the door and ushered him inside. Sang was not as quiet as he thought, but Su Yang had an unfair advantage when it came to the senses. Like many of the crew, he was not human. He was an old sea dog, a werewolf that was just over a century old. Sang had wondered what he was considering his vast knowledge. Finally, having an answer to why he always avoided anything silver was good.

Once inside, Sang explained the best that he could about what had happened just an hour ago between him and Ivy. It was as if he was a spectator in his own body, and then he had control again. Su Yang is concerned at first, then dismissed the issues as trauma and a possible concussion, both of which just needed time to heal properly. However, Sang could tell that the old wolf was holding something back. For now, he would let it go.

"Please, teach. Show me?" Sang tried in English for the first time. He pointed at the bands on Su Yang's wrists that held his needles.

"Again, with this?" Su Yang replied, surprised.

He shook his head, but Sang remained undeterred. He was adamant about learning the art.

"Please, teach. Show me," he tried again, this time more forcefully. "Please."

"All right, I have to tell Ivy."

Sang's eyes went wide at the mention of her name. "No, please. No tell. Secret?"

"Not from my captain," he replied.

Sang grabbed Su Yang by the shoulders and shook him. "Please, teach. No tell," he pleaded.

Though he was old, Su Yang was still fairly spry. He quickly removed Sang's hands from his shoulders, and, using just the knuckles of his index and middle fingers, he struck Sang in different places on his upper body. Sang felt his arms go limp and that he had no control over them as they fell to his sides. Surprised that Su Yang would attack him, suddenly broke Sang. He fell to his knees and looked up at Su Yang, who was standing casually, but Sang could see the coiling of his muscles as they readied themselves for a fight.

With tears welling in his eyes, Sang tried again. "Please, teach. No tell," he cried. "Please, help."

Su Yang sighed heavily. He must have thought him to be pathetic in that moment, Sang thought as he continued to cry and plead for help softly.

"Fine," Su Yang said after a few moments, quieting him and standing him back up.

He struck Sang in the same places rapidly, and Sang could feel and move his arms again. Though the movements were quick, Sang caught where they were that time. He kept the fact that he noticed to himself. Rotating his shoulders to clear the tingling feeling that was left

behind, Sang took the seat Su Yang offered to him. Su
Yang continued to stand, his arms folded over his chest.

"Why?" Su Yang asked.

It was such a simple word, and yet Sang did not fully
understand it. The confusion must have shown on his face
because Su Yang switched back to Mandarin to ask why
he wanted to learn acupuncture so badly. Sang gave him
an honest answer, his truth. Su Yang rubbed at his chin
where a fine stubble had grown in. It was a mix of black
and white. He had taken a few moments to think on
Sang's answer before answering him. Sang was hopeful as
he scrubbed the remaining tears from his face.

"I will teach you acupuncture and strengthen your
English, but I dislike keeping secrets from my captain.
Speak of this to no one and I will teach you," he said,
finally pointing to his wristbands.

"I get?" he asked, gesturing to his bare wrists.

"No, not yet. When I say you are ready."

He turned away from a disappointed Sang to rummage
through the many drawers he had in his cabinet fixed to
the wall around a desk. When he found what he was
looking for, he presented it to Sang. It was a strange
looking set of scrolls, old ones. They all had different
drawings with writing that he and Su Yang were probably
the only ones capable of reading. The first one had a man

on it and different lines pointing to different places on his extended arm. Each line had a unique description of where they pointed, ending in a small circle that followed a long, curved line along the arm, connecting to each circle. Su Yang showed Sang the other scrolls, each a different part of the body.

"You learn," Su Yang said to him, his tone stern.

Sang nodded, excited to learn something he thought was interesting and would be useful. Before he could finish going over the charts, Su Yang snatched them and quickly put them away.

"There you are," came a familiar, but groggy, voice.

"Good morning, Captain," Su Yang smiled.

Sang turned to see Ivy was up and looking more flushed than usual. He followed Su Yang's example and stood to greet her.

"Good morning, Captain," he repeated, mimicking Su Yang the best he could. His words came out clumsy, but he was happy he got them out.

"Ah, I see. English lessons going well?"

"As well as expected of a Korean child that speaks Mandarin," Su Yang replied.

She nodded. She still looked worse for wear. What all did he do to her?

"Well, you can finish them later. It's time for his combat training with the twins," she said, beckoning him to follow her as she left.

Sang hesitated, waiting for Su Yang to give him the go ahead. The old wolf had a look of pity on his face as he sent Sang along after her. Sang really was not a fighter.

# CHAPTER 10

Sang's training that morning went better this time. He only had to be killed twice. He was improving and showing an aptitude for combat, but he lacked the will to hurt others outside of defending himself. Even then, he was reluctant to strike back. Something was holding him back, and whatever it was, it needed to be removed. Ivy needed her dragon to be strong.

"So, how's he fairing?"

"He is improving, but still has a long way to go before he will be of any use in an actual fight.," Kuasa said.

"At least he stopped dying," Ivy pointed out.

"For now. Speaking of death, you are looking flushed. I thought the dragon was the only one that turned that color," she smiled. "Rought night?"

"And morning," Ivy admitted, blushing.

"Ah, that is why he is full of vigor."

"I suppose. But I honestly don't know what got into him. I just wish it would translate into his fighting."

Kuasa nodded. "Does he know how to use his fire properly?"

"You would have to ask him that. He won't take my blood."

They continued to monitor Kamau and Sang as they sparred. Sang had gained some sense of rhythm, at least enough to avoid Kamau's attacks, but he was mimicking at best. Maybe the twins' style of fighting did not suit him. Kuasa had taken up learning how to use a spear and a staff recently, and she did very well with them. Maybe Sang could learn as well.

"Captain?" Kuasa had been trying to get Ivy's attention, but had no luck until she placed her hand on her arm. "Are you sure you are well?"

"Hm? Oh, yes. I'm fine."

Kuasa narrowed her eyes at Ivy. Ivy could tell the taller woman did not believe her.

"I'm just a little worn out from my own sparring. That's all, I swear."

Kuasa grumbled, but let it go. She was right to be worried, however, but Ivy did not want anyone, especially her crew, to worry about her.

"By the way," Kuasa started. "The King of Tides is still expecting to see you. We can only stall for so long before he thinks we are ignoring his summons and sends someone out to retrieve us."

Ivy paled at that, but caught herself when Sang looked over at her. He barely dodged Kamau's attack in time.

"You let me worry about him," Ivy said.

"It is not him I am worried about," Kuasa replied.

"Drop it, Kuasa," she warned lightly. "Please."

Kuasa held up her hands in a mock surrender.

"All right, that's enough practice for the day. We need to get going," Ivy called out. "Don't want to keep his majesty waiting."

It took four days to reach the island that the King of Tides made his own and called home. Alexander Tempest was one of four sea kings, and the one that was most disliked by the other three. He was often a menace to them, frequently sacking their ships for no reason other than he could. Tempest was ex-military, and he served on a prison ship as the quartermaster, but he did not like the way the ship was being run and caused a mutiny. Killed the captain and freed the prisoners. Once they caught him, the court sentenced him to hang, but he escaped by persuading a weak-willed guard to let him go.

His silver tongue and unnatural charisma led him to start a cult consisting of escaped convicts and pirates. Forming his own crew, he obtained multiple ships to spread his influence and gather followers. He was born half water elemental and half incubus, and had a bad habit of dry-land drowning those he did not like.

Tempest met Ivy when she was just thirteen and impressionable. He taught her how to use her succubus nature when she came into her powers at sixteen. It did not take too many years before she wanted to captain her own ship. As a reward for her loyalty and strong command skills, he gifted her the Pale Emperor, an English galleon warship, and the first ship he captured. Because of his feud with the King of Stars and Nightmares, Tempest kept himself barricaded on his island, surrounded by his best fighters and his vast harem.

Once they arrived, Ivy gave the order for everyone to stay on the ship and to keep Sang hidden and safe. She would meet the devil alone.

"Ivy, how good of you to come home. I thought I was going to have to send Jack to get you," Tempest smiled.

"Please," Ivy scoffed. "I'm more than he can handle. He could never best me in a fight."

Tempest's smile turned into a smirk. "I'm not so sure about that. It's been years since your last scrap with him. He's improved his skills since." He lounged on his throne; his long leg thrown casually over the plush arm. "He wants a rematch."

He was a cocky man. Ivy hated that about him. Among other things. He was a foul bastard, even if he was easy on the eyes. Alexander Tempest was a tall, lean man with long, black hair that ran just past his shoulders. He had reddish brown eyes that were always lined in thick black liner, pale pink lips, and nearly translucent white skin. Even Ivy was not as pale as him, and she was a dhampir. His lack of pigmentation may have been because of his spending nearly all of his time indoors and in his cave. When they used to sail together, he would spend most of his time in his quarters, usually in bed with her or his newest conquest. There was always one close by. He had an insatiable lust that could rival any pure-blooded incubus.

"He can have his rematch whenever he likes," Ivy started, making sure she sounded confident. "I'll gladly break his other arm," she purred.

Tempest roared with laughter. "That's my girl." He paused a moment, examining her. "So, tell me. What new toys have you brought for me?"

She splayed her hands out at her sides. "Sorry, couldn't find anything you would like." Ivy hated having to bring him people to add to his harem, but it was the only way to keep her ship and crew... and her own freedom.

He made a tsking sound. "Oh Ivy, you sell yourself too short." He waved someone out from the shadows. Ivy turned to see Lizzy, her old rival for his affections. Lizzy sauntered past Ivy with a cheshire grin as she went to sit in Tempest's lap. It was all Ivy could do not to gag when they kissed, his hand going into her already loose blouse to cup her breast. Lizzy moaned into his deepening kiss as she stroked his cock through the material of his trousers. When he released the young shapeshifter, he left her breathless and wanting, her ample breasts heaving from her arousal. Ivy could smell it on both of them.

"What's with the face, Ivy? What did you expect would happen when you left me to captain my ship? Someone has to keep my bed warm, especially since the toys you bring me break so easily."

"Like I said, you're a hard man to please," Ivy replied.

"True enough, but no one could please me as well as you did. Though not for a lack of trying," he said, squeezing Lizzy's face.

He grabbed her around the waist when she tried to get out of his lap. She was pouting as usual, but stopped struggling. He spread her legs wide and pushed her skirt aside. She gasped, then started moaning again when his long, nimble fingers found their prize. His other hand continued to play with her breast. The air was thick with lust, and Ivy was having a hard time containing her own arousal.

"You see, Lizzy here, with all her endowments, just can't satisfy me the way you did." He shushed her when she protested, burying his face in the space between her neck and shoulder, but maintained eye contact with Ivy. "However, she looks enough like you when I fuck her from behind, and that's almost good enough." He tightened his grip on her as he continued to finger fuck her. "Sometimes, I make her turn into you just so I can get off."

Ivy saw what looked like shame on Lizzy's face, the hint of tears starting in her eyes as Tempest pushed her off of him and onto the stone floor of the cave he made into his lair. He had a large house that he stayed in; it was heavily fortified, but he always held meetings in the large cave nearby. Lizzy gathered herself and scurried off.

"You're an asshole!" Ivy growled, her fists tightly at her sides.

Tempest only laughed. "Also true."

"What did you want, Tempest? Why did you call me back her?"

The amusement left his face. "Watch your tone, or my toys won't be the only thing I break," he warned.

He had a way of being threatening without being loud and aggressive.

"Sorry. Why did you call me here?"

"First, why did you lie to me earlier?" he asked calmly.

"I didn't."

"You're lying to me again, Ivy. You know I don't like being lied to."

"I don't know what you're talking about," she said through gritted teeth.

"A little birdie told me you found something valuable that I would like," he said casually.

She narrowed her eyes at him. "I don't—" Her eyes went wide. "No!"

"Ah, there it is. That look."

"You can't have him!" she growled.

"I can, and I will have him," he smiled. "And you will give him to me freely."

"Never. He's part of my crew. He's mine."

"Oh? Either I get my dragon, or you lose your ship and crew."

"You wouldn't."

"What in our history together makes you think I won't? Now bring me my dragon."

Ivy stood there for a few moments, trying to quell her rage. How did he find out about Sang? No one in her crew would dare tell him. She handpicked them all; they were loyal to her. At least, she thought.

"Ivy," he sang. "I'm waiting."

Ivy bowed her head, then turned to leave. She held her head high, despite the bitter taste of bile in her mouth. She would find her traitor. And may the gods help them when she did.

She was still fuming when she got back to the ship. Sang was not ready for a man like Tempest. The boy was still far too weak mentally and physically, but there was nothing she could do for him now. She had hoped to keep him hidden until he became more formidable, but he was lost to her now. Ivy had no leverage to win his freedom.

"Captain?" spoke Kuasa. "Are you all right? Your face is very red and twisted."

"No, I'm not all right," she replied, trying and failing to calm herself, but the more her thoughts lingered on the subject, the angrier she got. In a fit of rage, she punched the side wall of the ship, splintering the wood. "Fuck!"

"What did that bastard want from you this time?" Kuasa asked, bewildered by the outburst.

Ivy fell to her knees, breaking down into angry tears. She roared with frustration. It got everyone's attention and her quartermaster, Dutch, came over to see what was going on.

"What happened?" he asked.

Kuasa shrugged. She was equally interested.

"For goodness' sake, pull yourself together, girl," Dutch said sternly. "What did he want?"

With Kuasa's help, Ivy got back to her feet. She wiped her face with the handkerchief Dutch offered before speaking. "He knows about Sang," she said, after a moment. "He wants my dragon."

Dutch clicked his teeth. "Really? Is that all? Is that what has you blubbering on your knees?"

Ivy scowled at him, but he did not back down.

"You are Black Ivy Thatch. You put fear in the hearts of men and women. And you command the Pale Emperor, not Tempest," he fussed. "The boy is part of this crew now, your crew. Tempest can't take him from you."

"I can either hand him over or lose all of you, ship included," she countered. "Don't think for a second that I wasn't willing to fight for him."

"I told you; you should just let me kill him," said Kuasa.

"If it were that easy, I would have done it myself," said Dutch. "You and your brother wouldn't stand a chance. Not even in a fair fight. And she can't afford to lose either of you," he explained. He turned his focus back to Ivy. "How did he even find out about him?"

"We have a leak on the ship," she growled.

"Then I will plug it. For now, let him have the boy. We'll get him back soon enough."

Ivy nodded reluctantly, then went to retrieve Sang with Kuasa close behind.

Sang was confused when Ivy took him off the ship. The twins followed them, both with serious looks on their faces. That was a normal look for Kuasa, but not Kamau. It worried Sang. They reached a large cave opening near the beach. Along the outside of the cave, in an alcove, was what looked like a shrine. The entrance seemed vast as they passed through it. The textured walls appeared to be painted where the reflected light of the sun hit them. Ivy had to move him along as he stopped to marvel at the wonder and beauty of the inside of the cave.

The deeper they went, the more people he was seeing. He moved closer to Ivy the more he was stared at. He wanted to ask what was going on and why they were there, but he could not yet form the words correctly. When they finally reached where they intended, Sang saw a pale man lounging casually in a large chair that looked like it could fit at least two more people on it. The moment he saw Sang, he grinned devilishly and jumped out of the chair to meet them. Sang looked at his group and their faces looked filled with anger as the man approached. He got chills when the pale man stood in front of them. The man moved Ivy aside and stepped in front of him.

"Mm, he's a pretty thing. Frail looking, but delectable all the same," he said.

He turned his head to Ivy, who was still scowling.

"I can see why you want to keep him all to yourself." He returned his attention to Sang, gently cupping his face. "Do you have any idea how much I can fuck him and not have to worry about killing him?" He squeezed Sang's face, making him struggle. "At least not permanently, anyway."

Upon his release, Sang lost his balance and Kamau swiftly caught him. He could only make out some of what he said, and Sang did not like any of it. Sang wanted to leave as soon as possible. He tugged at Ivy's sleeve, but she ignored him and brushed his hand away.

"Don't hurt him," Ivy spoke through gritted teeth.

The pale man laughed. "He's mine now. I can do whatever I want to him. And I will," he said, turning to walk back to his enormous chair. "Do whatever I want to him, I mean. It's going to be so much fun. I love when I get new toys to play with."

With no effort, he sat back down and got comfortable.

"I will get him back," Ivy said. She had her fists tight at her sides.

"Really? And how is that?" he asked, tilting his head curiously.

"You're going to need me to do something awful for you eventually, or I'll find something you want more."

The pale man grinned. "It's funny you say that. I do have a job for you."

"I'll do it if you promise to give him back unharmed."

"We'll see. I want you to locate a ship."

"That's all?" she scoffed.

"This is a special ship. I need you to get to it before it reaches its destination and take the treasure it holds," he explained.

"Sounds simple."

"Oh, and leave no survivors. You'll sink the ship if you know what's good for you."

Ivy narrowed her eyes. "This sounds too easy. Why not send Jack?"

"It won't be easy, and like you said, you're good at what you do. Besides, you want something from me."

"Fine. Whose ship is it?"

"So many questions. You should get moving if you want to catch them. Lizzy will give you all the details."

"Kuasa, Kamau, let's go." She turned to leave, the twins behind her.

When Sang tried to follow, he found he could not move. He cried out after Ivy, but she continued to ignore him.

"Oh no, you're not going anywhere," said the pale man.

Sang turned his head the best he could to see that the pale man had his hand outstretched towards him.

"You're mine now," he grinned.

A tear fell from Sang's eye as he watched helplessly as Ivy and the twins walked out of his view. He had been betrayed. She had promised him freedom and was now abandoning him to a man he did not know. The pale man gave him bad feelings, and he had no desire to be left alone with him. When Sang turned back to the pale man, the pale man had a sinister look in his ink-lined eyes. Not even Leung caused Sang to shake as badly as he was then. Nothing good would happen if he stayed there.

Sang was not much of a fighter, and killing did not sit well with him, but he would escape this place somehow. He wished he knew more about what he was. He should have learned to at least control fire by now, but he did not want to hurt Kuasa or Kamau. Cultivating the ability also required blood, which also meant hurting someone. Though he had taken three lives, it was not in him to be violent, but he would not be someone's slave again.

"I wonder. What's going on in that pretty head?"

Sang glared at the man, swearing at him in Mandarin.

The pale man's lip curled up in a sneer. "That is an ugly language. Never let me hear it again."

Sang's eyes widened in bewilderment when his body moved on its own. He fought to control it as he stiffly walked towards the pale man. No matter how hard he fought, he could not stop until he reached him. The pale man leaned forward, staring Sang deep in the eyes.

"You're not much of a dragon, are you? Either way, I'm going to enjoy breaking you in," he purred.

Sang did not understand, but he knew to be afraid. When the pale man clinched his fist, Sang's eyes went wide again, and he screamed. It was as if his blood moved faster through his veins before they burst. His screams grew louder when bloody spikes pierced his skin from the inside out. When he collapsed to the hard, cold ground, he could feel his body dying as the pale male laughed. Blinking slowly as he gasped for his last breaths, Sang felt no pain as the fire consumed him whole.

When he reformed, he was immediately picked up and put in chains that burned him by men he did not know. They put him on his knees in front of the pale man, and the pale man smiled wickedly down at him.

The pale man lifted Sang's chin with a single finger. "My name is Alexander Tempest, the King of Tides, and you belong to me."

Sang shook, his chains rattling with the motion. He had never experienced death or pain like that. Death was staring him in the face and smiling. All hope of escape had left him.

# CHAPTER 11

The gentle sea breeze and the light crashing of the waves against the ship's hull did nothing to calm her or ease her worry. Guilt consumed her for leaving Sang with that monster, but she prioritized the safety and wellbeing of her crew over the consequences the boy would suffer. Tempest still blamed her for the death of the last dragon. She blamed herself as well, though she had nothing to do with him not coming back. All Andr disappeared that day, but then Sang appeared after so many years. She leaned forward on the ship's bow and sighed. She would get him back, no matter how long it took.

So engrossed in her thoughts, she missed the call that a ship had been sighted.

"Captain!" Dutch called. "Get your head on straight."

Ivy barely reacted to being yelled at. She straightened herself out before giving the order to raise the bloody flag. They were close enough to fire on the other vessel, an East Indiaman, from the looks of her.

"Prepare yourselves for a fight, lads! Let's show 'em what the crew of the Pale Emperor is made of!" She drew her sword and raised it high. "Give no quarter!"

The crew shouted their approval, and when she lowered her sword toward the target vessel, they roared. The other ship showed no signs of surrendering, but had no interest in fighting either. Despite the appearance of slowness, the Pale Emperor gave chase when the other ship turned to run.

When they caught the other ship, they boarded her. The other crew was ready for a fight this time.

"Find the treasure and leave no survivors," Ivy ordered. "But leave their captain to me."

It did not take her long to find the other captain. He had cut down two of her men before confronting her.

"Do you know whose ship this is?" he asked through gritted teeth.

"No," Ivy laughed, then kicked him in the gut. "And I don't care."

When he lunged at her with his cutlass, she stepped to his left side and tripped him, sending him to the floor. The moment he rolled over, she ran her sword through his throat. Once she was sure the entire crew of the enemy ship was dead, she went in search of the treasure that warranted having a ship full of people murdered.

"Captain," Kuasa called, covered in blood. "We found what they were hiding below. It is not treasure."

Ivy growled, sheathing her sword. She did not like killing for no reason. "Is there anything of value on this ship?"

"It's just a boy, Captain," Kuasa explained.

Kamau forcibly removed the boy from the room where he had barricaded himself. He did not look over sixteen or seventeen years old. He had long brown hair pulled back into a ponytail and bright blue eyes. Whoever he was, he wore fine clothes. Ivy thought it strange that the crew of the ship would risk their lives over a slip of a boy.

"Shit! Tie him up and bring him along," she ordered, turning to walk away.

"My da will see ya all hang for this!" the boy shouted in a slight Irish accent. "Release me at once!"

Ivy narrowed her eyes at the boy. He did not sound like a boy. She went over to him and ripped his shirt, revealing the binding over the chest.

"Fuck! You're a girl. Where's your governess?" Ivy growled.

"The dark one killed her for tryin' to protect me," she replied, struggling against Kamau's hold. "Let me go, you stupid animal!"

Ivy slapped the girl hard for her remark. "And put a gag on her while you're at it," Ivy called back, ascending the stairs.

The girl was clearly a noble's child. What was Tempest thinking? Did he plan to ransom her back to her parents? That would be out of character for him. She would get her answers and her dragon back.

Blood splattered across Tempest's face again as he gleefully pulled another of what looked like crushed gems on a scale from the boy's body. The boy screamed in agony while his shoulders were being stripped of each scale, one by one. Tempest handed each one that he pulled to Jack, one of his most loyal captains and trusted second in command. Jack did not look at all bothered by what Tempest was doing. If anything, he looked bored. Tempest appreciated him for his indifference to his methods of controlling others. Tempest did not like to see weakness in others, especially from those that worked for him. He was going to tame this dragon just as he did the last one, and Jack would bear witness to it.

Once he had removed all the small scales from the Andr's shoulders, he flipped him onto his back while he cried and begged in a language Tempest did not care for. He straddled the boy once more as he ripped out the small scales that lined his abdomen, wondering if any of them would grow back. The skin where the scales had been removed had turned bloodied and raw, with small, wet tendrils splayed out where the scales were pulled from. Tempest marveled at the sight.

"Sir, what is the point of taking these?" asked Jack, holding up the bloody pile of green-tinted black scales in his hands.

Tempest stopped mid pull to address Jack, the tendrils still attached to the scale. The scales Jack held looked like blood-stained emeralds under the torchlight. They were beautiful. "Two reasons," he started, pulling the scale out and handing it to Jack. It was like pulling the legs off a spider. "One," he said, pulling out another, "is to break the subject down, so that I can make him strong, or at least compliant," he explained. "And two." He pulled out another and smiled at the extra loud howl the boy let out as it echoed throughout the cave. "I think they're pretty. You know how I love pretty things."

Tempest watched as Jack stood there with no real expression on his face as he accepted another scale. Jack turned and dumped the pile he had into a bucket before wiping his hands of the blood. Tempest had insisted that Jack hold the scales with his hands first and did not bother to tell him why. And Jack did not ask why, he just did it. Jack was cold-hearted, and Tempest liked that about him. They were both sadistic in their own ways. Tempest more so than Jack, but Jack had his moments. But Jack was a human amongst monsters, and all humans had their limits. And Tempest was going to test them. He offered Jack the bloodied pliers, but Jack respectfully declined. Jack did not want to interrupt Tempest's fun. Tempest shrugged, then continued to rip out more scales that led to the boy's groin area.

He found he enjoyed the sounds of tearing flesh as he removed each scale, the faint smell of sulfur and copper filling his nostrils. The top of the scales were rough against his fingertips, and the bottoms were slick. The blood was a lovely red hue under the firelight, a stark contrast against Tempest's nearly translucent skin. He pulled every small scale from the front of the boy's body before moving on to the back of him. He lightly touched the green-tinted black feathers at the nape of the boy's neck, then tore them all out with his hand.

The Andr screamed and flailed beneath Tempest as he took every small scale that ran along the sides of the larger, more bejeweled, armored plates down his spine. He thought about taking those as well, and selling them, but decided not to. The last thing that he needed was an Andr in a berserker rage in a cave. And taking the spinal plates just might be the thing that triggers him into such a rage.

He looked down at the Andr. He was a beautiful mess covered in all that blood, with patches of indents in his skin from where the scales once were. Standing up, he pulled the crying boy to his knees, then put one hand at the top of his head and the other under his chin. He looked directly at Jack, and then violently twisted the boy's head sideways. The sobbing stopped abruptly, and Jack did not flinch. Tempest dropped the body and quickly stepped away as lovely green flames covered the boy like hundreds of butterflies descending onto a carcass. It was a beautiful sight to behold.

Some time had passed before there was movement in the husk that was left behind by the fire. When he saw the scales had indeed grown back, Tempest got excited. He would have another set. This dragon was going to be far more entertaining than the last one. He found he looked forward to all the screams.

The voyage back to the island of the King of Tides felt longer than a few days. Ivy was anxious and irritated. She was pissed to have been sent out on a fool's errand, but it would be worth it to get Sang back. Hopefully, he would forgive her for leaving him with such a vicious creature.

The moment they made landfall, Ivy was off the ship. Kuasa and Kamau were close behind with the heavily protesting girl they had captured. Ivy headed straight for the cave. Tempest would likely still be there so he could be near water while playing with his new 'toy'. It was the safest option when dealing with a fire-breathing dragon. Even if he did not know how to use his power. Sang was especially vulnerable with a sadistic water demon.

When she saw Tempest, he was lounging on his throne while one of his toys pleasured him orally. However, what immediately got her attention was the new, glittery piece of jewelry around his neck. It was a bib style collar with black trinkets that had an emerald green tint to them. There were enough of them to nearly cover his bare chest. They were all held together by metal chain links that covered his neck and shoulder. Her eyes went wide with the realization of what they were. Dragon scales. He had ripped off many of Sang's scales that were on random patches of his skin all over his body.

"What did you do?" Ivy growled, her hand at her sword.

Tempest looked up at her and smiled ruefully. "Oh, this? I just had it made," he said, with one hand in the long, black hair of his bobbing toy and the other at his collar. "I pulled them myself," he grinned, before releasing his load into the mouth of the slave servicing him.

The light caught on something that glittered on the slave, and when Tempest grabbed a fist full of their hair to pull them off him, Ivy saw their face when Tempest cast them aside. Sang fell to the ground, cum streaming from his open mouth. He was panting, and he appeared barely conscious. All the life had gone out of his eyes.

"I'll kill you!" Ivy roared, but she found she could not move.

"Ah, ah, ah," he smiled. He immobilized Kuasa and Kamau as well, with another gesture of his free hand. "We had a deal. Remember?"

Ivy screamed in frustration.

"Calm down, he's fine... for now. Did you bring me what I wanted?"

"Yes," she hissed. "Now give him back to me."

"I don't think I will."

"We had a deal!" she screamed, fighting back tears.

"Do you know who that girl is?" he asked, genuinely interested.

Ivy only glared at him.

"That is the only child of the King of Stars and Nightmares. How do you think he'll react when he finds out that kidnapped his only child?"

"I did it for you!"

"No, you did it for him," he said, pointing at Sang. "You could have said no," he chuckled.

Again, she growled. "You bastard."

"You also murdered the crew escorting her to him, so that's another strike against you."

"I can take her back and explain things."

"He'll still kill you for the crew you murdered, but I can protect you."

"And what will that cost?"

"I get the girl and I'm keeping the dragon," he smiled slyly.

"I refuse."

"It is absolutely adorable that you think you have a choice." He leaned forward on his throne, his hands still outstretched towards the quartet. "You can either leave with your lives, or," he clenched his fists, sending them screaming to the ground, "you can die here."

He released his hold on them, leaving them gasping for air. Ivy looked over at Sang. He had sat up and stared at them with a vacant look in his eyes. What all had Tempest done to him? As far as she could see, he still had his scales, at least on his torso. Tempest had him dressed in nothing more than a long skirt with high slits on either side. There was no recognition or life in his eyes. In a matter of days, Tempest broke Sang. Even if she got him back, he would never forgive her.

"So, what will it be?"

Ivy looked up at Tempest with disgust and rage in her eyes. "I will end you for this. Mark my words."

"Of course you will. We all have dreams," he grinned. "Now, get off my island, but don't go too far. It's not going to be safe for you, and I may have need of you later."

Before she could respond, he shooed them away. The poor girl they were leaving behind went pale and struggled against her new captures, but Tempest was a sadist that enjoyed causing pain, and he made a gesture with his hand. The girl howled out, collapsing into unconsciousness. Ivy left with her tail between her legs. The girl was as lost to her as Sang was. Now, she and her crew were in danger because of her poor leadership, but she would fix it, even if it meant sacrificing her own life.

She ordered the twins to stay behind to watch Tempest, but to stay out of sight. Ivy wanted revenge, and she needed more information before she could see to it. She would make sure that her crew was safe from now on, but the King of Tides needed to die.

# CHAPTER 12

T empest was elated to have a new toy to play with. The dragon was becoming lifeless and needed a break. So, he moved on to break in his new plaything. Her name was Sinead, and she had the creamiest skin he had seen in a while, not since Aine. He had loved Aine; she was the most beautiful woman he had come across in decades. She was a weak human that had spurned his affections in favor of another. The old memories angered him. Now he needed to work out his rising aggression.

Before he could exercise his personal demons, a servant came in and handed him a letter that had been sent by raven. Tempest opened the letter, a smirk gracing his face as he read it. He forcefully pulled the chain and brought Sinead, who was attached to it, over to his throne. He forced her to her knees as he sat down. With a light tap on her nose with the rolled-up message, he regarded her thoughtfully for a moment. She had clear blue eyes, and he found he wanted to pluck them from her face for the look of contempt she was giving him. She would learn her place soon enough, so he left them as they were for now. He wondered how her eyes would change as he trained her.

"Do you know what this is?" he asked, holding up the letter.

"How should Oi know?" she replied, scowling still.

"Well, it's a summons. A meeting of the four kings of the sea has been called," he explained.

She continued to scowl at him.

"You're probably wondering if you should care, right? I'll tell you why." He stood then, looming over her. "Your daddy is one of the four kings, and he wants you back," he grinned, leaning forward.

Her eyes perked up at that. He could see the hope in them.

"But," he started, getting closer to her face, "I'm not giving you back."

He grinned as he watched the hope drain out of her eyes.

"You have to give me back. He's a sea king. He'll kill you," she growled out.

Tempest laughed at that. "He can try, but I am also a sea king. The King of Tides," he exclaimed.

She covered her mouth to conceal a gasp. "You're the one who—"

"Yes," he snapped, still smiling. "I'm that king." He grabbed her by the face and squeezed hard. "Now, you're going to be a good little girl, or end up like your mother." He let her go to sit back down.

"You're a monster!"

"Yes. What else would a sea king be?" he asked, splaying his hands out to the sides. "And if you don't watch your tongue, I'll cut it from your head," he said. "Then again, I could find a better use for it while it's still in your head," he grinned deceptively. He checked his pocket watch and looked over the letter again. "I've got time before I have to leave." He got back up and went over to her, squatting down. "How about we have a little fun? Give me a proper sendoff."

He bared his fangs at her and caught her by the throat when she tried to move away. Tempest could smell her fear, taste it on his tongue, and it aroused him that much more. He was going to claim every part of her as his. His Aine had the same look in her eyes before he took her.

He was out of it as they dragged him onto a ship. It had been many days since he had been on one; he had lost count of how long he had been on that island. He had not seen the sun since they abandoned him there. It was painfully bright after being in a dark cave for so long. Though, by now, he should have been used to being kept in dark places. The chains around his wrists still burned, but he was getting used to the pain. It was not so bad if he did not move around much.

The pale man that introduced himself as Alexander Tempest, the King of Tides, liked to keep Sang close to sate his lust whenever it came up. Which was all the time, it seemed. Sang had resisted, even attempted to fight back with what he had learned from the twins, but Tempest was strong. Too Strong. Tempest repeatedly killed and beat Sang until he finally submitted to his twisted desires.

He was as lifeless as a doll by the time Tempest was done with him.

Sang did not know where they were going, but it took a couple of days to get there. They led him by his chains into a large stone building. Once inside, something stirred in Sang. He caught a somewhat familiar scent that caused him to shake and stop all movement. It did not help that he thought he saw shadows move freely around them. The shadows were all different in size and shape, with blazing white eyes. Some were small and cute, looking like strange animals. He saw one bite the shadow of a random person near it, then devoured the shadow completely. The man that was now without a shadow turned as white as a sheet before he fell dead to the floor. With eyes wide open, Sang tried to turn and run, but the person holding his chains prevented him from getting far. He struggled as they pulled him forward, but stopped when he got Tempest's attention. He went still for a moment before moving forward again.

Tempest continued to lead the way into a large open room that had a wide, circular table with four chairs. Tempest sat in one with Sang standing behind him while the one called Jack held onto his chains. Others filed into the room, including a woman that smelled like Leung. Sang shook again as she took the seat to the right of

Tempest, with two others standing at her sides a few feet back. She made eye contact with Sang and smiled at him as she petted a demonic shadow eating creature in her lap. There was something cruel in her eyes that reminded him of Leung's wife. It concerned him she might realize who he was and try to take him back to Leung, but that might be better than his current situation.

A rather large, bearded man sat down at Tempest's left with two men behind him. He held a coin in his palm, and Sang watched as the coin floated in the air mere inches above his palm. The coin shook in the air as it morphed into many different shapes rapidly. It amazed Sang, and scared him a little, especially since the bearded man kept forming different weapons and glaring at Tempest. Tempest just leaned back in his chair and smiled.

The last to take a seat, the one across from Tempest, looked as if it was taking everything in him not to walk over and end Tempest's life in the worst way possible. Sang hoped that he would do just that. There was so much power flaring in the room that Sang felt strangled by it. All he wanted to do was curl up somewhere he could not be seen or heard.

"I suggest you calm yourself, Doyle. We're on neutral ground," Tempest said, drilling the tip of a dagger into the wood of the table.

"Oi'll gut ye fer what ye done, Tempest," said the angry man.

He had a funny accent when he spoke. Sang did not completely understand what he was saying because of it, but it was a pleasant and interesting sound.

"After what you did, we might let him," said the Chinese woman to his right.

Three of them continued to argue, and Sang was unsure of what was going on. It sounded as if two of them were angry at Tempest, who continued to smile and speak calmly as if he knew something they did not. The large, bearded man snatched his coin out of the air and slammed his fist on the table, getting everyone's attention.

"Enough!" he shouted. "You're kings of the sea. Stop bickering like children."

The sound of his voice made the room shake, but Sang felt the earth beneath him rumble as well. He wondered what manner of monster could move the earth. It was all he could do to stop his own body from shaking.

"Take care of yer pet, Tempest. He looks like he's about to shit himself," the man with the accent said, sitting back down.

Sang stiffened when Tempest turned his head to him and made a gesture with his hand, but then decided not to. He had a cruel smile on his face, but Sang knew that there would be pain later. Tempest did not like weakness in the presences of others.

Tempest turned back to face the others. To his right sat Wan Shǎndiàn, the King of Storms. She was half lightning elemental and half Vanita—a shadow eater. She could create shades, small minions that would devour the shadows of others for her to absorb for more power. The more shadows they ate, the bigger the shades would get. She was dangerous in the light.

To his left sat Jones Davies, the King of the Depths. Davies was half earth elemental and half Gwragedd Annwn. He had command of the earth in all its forms, as well as water. He had a habit of creating islands whenever he would raise a sunken ship for its treasure. Though he was fully capable of parting the sea to get to the ships, it weakened him considerably, and he could never hold the sea at bay for very long.

And sitting directly in front of Tempest was Donovan Doyle, the King of Stars and Nightmares. He was half air elemental and half Umbra. While in the presence of the King of Storms, he kept his shadow dormant as it was a highly prized target for the Vanita. However, Doyle directed his focus towards Tempest. They had been enemies for a long time because they fell in love with the same woman. Tempest failed to gain her affections, so he killed her, but not before she gave birth to the daughter he was now holding hostage.

"Can we get to why we're all here? I have better things I could be doing. My pet, for instance," Tempest said, reclining in his chair again and grinning.

"Give me back me daughter, ye bastard!" Doyle roared.

"I don't know what you're talking about," Tempest smiled.

"Don't be a fool, Alexander," started Davies. "Give the girl back and pay for the loss of the crew you murdered."

Tempest just continued to smile.

"Are ye tryin' ta start a war, Tempest?" asked Doyle.

"Careful, Doyle. Wan's pets look a little hungry," said Tempest.

Wan scoffed. "My 'pets' are fine, but you will not be if you do not return Donovan's daughter."

"We're trying to maintain peace, Tempest," said Davies. "What are you playing at?"

"Nothing. Doyle owes me a woman and a crew. Or did we all forget that he stole my woman and sank one of my ships?"

"Are ye daft? Ye knew she didn't want ye, and ye killed her fer it!"

"You cannot be serious! All this over the affections of a woman that did not want you?" asked Wan, appalled.

Tempest's lip curled up in a sneer. "Doyle poisoned her against me."

"Oi poisoned her? She saw ye fer what ye are. A monster. Now ye take me only daughter. The only thin' Oi have ta remember me Aine by."

Tempest started smiling again before he spoke again. "And she's the spitting image of her mother… in every way."

"Don't ye touch her!" Doyle roared again, jumping out of his seat and pulling a blade from inside his coat.

Tempest threw his head back and laughed as Doyle's men held him back. Even his shadow got involved, but Wan's shades became agitated, forcing his shadow to go back to being dormant.

"Enough!" shouted Davies, causing the room to shake again.

"Sit down, Doyle," said Tempest, barely containing his amusement. "Your little girl's a woman now, thanks to me, and she can hardly get enough of my cock."

"Oi'll kill ye fer what—"

"Yes, yes. You'll kill me fer what I done," Tempest interrupted, mocking the Irishman. He raised a brow when Doyle raised his hands and gestured towards him.

"I'll burst every blood vessel in your body before you can take all the air out of my lungs," he warned. "Now, sit down and hear my offer."

"What makes ye tink Oi want whatever ye have?" Doyle growled. "Oi want me little girl, nothin' else."

"Well, that's too bad. She's mine now. I've marked every inch of her a hundred times over now. I said sit down, Doyle," Tempest said firmly.

"Do as he says, Doyle. The girl's tainted now. Might as well let him keep her," said Davies.

"Agreed," said Wan.

There was a look of shock and disbelief on Doyle's face at the others siding with Tempest. He could feel Doyle's blood pressure rise as he shook with rage. He enjoyed seeing Doyle in such a state. Tempest knew there was nothing the King of Stars and Nightmares could do now. At least not without starting a war that would affect them all. Still, he would offer an olive branch. He was having fun, but he got his revenge on Doyle twice over. He would have to watch his back for sure now.

Doyle spat to the side before finally sitting back down. Glaring at Tempest, he said, "Whatever ye offerin' better be worth tha life o' me daughter."

Tempest leaned back in his chair, lacing his fingers together. "I offer you Ivy Thatch as a bride, and the Pale Emperor and its crew as her dowry."

"Oi don't want ye old whore fer a bride, but Oi'll take that dragon off ye hands," Doyle countered. "He don't look like much, but a dragon is a dragon."

"Him?" Tempest asked, pointing at Sang without looking. "Oh, I broke him, unfortunately. Didn't even take long. So, unless you're willing to fuck him, he'd be no use to you," he explained casually. "I suggest you accept my offer. Ivy would make a fine bride. She'll do everything she can to please you, and she is very good at pleasing men. If he spoke, the Andr would agree."

Wan narrowed her eyes. "China wants that dragon for the murder of his previous master's only son."

"That has nothing to do with me. Besides, he's mine now, and I'm not bored with him yet." Tempest was getting bored and irritated. He wanted to go home, not be in a room with an old whore, an old man that had nodded off, and his most hated rival. "So, what will it be, Doyle?"

Doyle took a few moments before he answered. "Fine, Oi'll take what yer offerin', but ye had better treat me li'l girl right."

"I'll treat her however I want. She's mine."

Doyle growled, "How'd ye feel if Oi treated yer Ivy like shit on me boot?"

Tempest had a look of indifference when he answered. "You can do with her as you please. I don't care either way. She's your problem now."

"That's why Aine didn't want ye. Ye be a devil."

"That's fair, but it doesn't matter now, does it?" he grinned.

Doyle only continued to glare at him.

"Now that we've concluded this bit of business, can we go? And can someone check to see if Davies is still alive?"

"One last thing, Alexander," said Wan.

Tempest regarded her with a look of exasperation. "Yes, madame? What else could you possibly want?"

"For one thing, cease behaving like a petulant child. And secondly, you will cease with sacking our ships, or Doyle and his shadow will be the least of your worries."

Tempest grinned broadly. "Do you really believe any of you are a threat to me?"

"I beg your pardon, boy?" said Wan, offended.

"Your shades eat shadow after shadow and you can barely summon a thunderbolt big enough to raise the hairs on my arms," Tempest started. "Doyle is the weakest of us. He couldn't even keep his daughter safe. And when was the last time the old man raised a ship from the depths? Seriously, is he even alive?"

"I'm not so old that I can't shatter every bone in that scrawny body of yours," said Davies, his arms folded over his broad chest and his eyes still closed.

Tempest narrowed his eyes suspiciously at Davies before returning his attention to the other two sea kings. "I'm doing Doyle a favor giving him the Emperor. Even if you were to join forces against me, I could still kill you all, but I haven't because I'm an honorable man and it amuses me keeping you all alive."

"Honorable? Ye haven't any honor, ye silver-tongued devil. Ye won't leave this place alive now," said Doyle.

"Won't I? You're not the only one with something they hold dear, Doyle. And if you think for one moment my captains won't take those things and destroy them, you're mistaken," Tempest started. "If my ravens don't get word to my captains in a certain amount of time, you all will lose everything."

"What did you do, Tempest?" roared Davies, opening his eyes finally.

Tempest smiled ear to ear. "Kill me and find out."

"Stop it! All of you!" said Wan. "We all know when he is serious."

Doyle cursed aloud.

"I'm leaving now," he said, standing. "I would say it's been a pleasure, but it really hasn't. Let's not do this again."

"Yer gonna pay fer what ye done, Tempest. Mark me words."

"I'm sure I will one day, but not today," Tempest smiled.

He walked out of the room with his Andr and second-in-command close behind.

# CHAPTER 13

"We have to leave his fleet!" shouted Dutch.

The rest of the crew shouted in agreement. They were all discussing getting out from under Tempest to strike out on their own. Especially after he set them all up against the King of Stars and Nightmares.

"There is no way he'll let us or the Emperor go," Ivy said. "He'd kill us all and sink the ship first."

"What if we plead our case to the other three sea kings? Surely they'll understand. None of them are fond of the King of Tides," spoke a crewman.

"Tempest is an evil man with the second largest fleet of the sea kings, and most of them are warships. The other kings have nothing to gain by helping us," Ivy explained. "We're on our own, but Tempest has his weaknesses, and I will kill him for everything he's done to us."

"How, if we don't have the other kings to help? We may be his strongest ship, but we're outnumbered," said another crewman.

"I know it looks hopeless, but we just need to bide our time," Ivy said, trying to reassure her crew and herself.

"That dragon would have been useful," spoke Dutch. "How he found out about him is still a mystery," he said to Ivy alone.

"Have you not found the mole?"

"Sorry, captain. I haven't. The crew is large, and there are a few fresh faces, but none of them were with Tempest and have nothing to gain by telling him anything."

"Word got to him somehow. It's entirely possible he had a spy on the island that we found him on," she guessed, but even she could not be sure of the loyalty of her crew anymore. She had let her feelings get the better of her, and now there were some rumblings about leaving her. However, she made a promise to get them all away from Tempest safely, but she would hold nothing against anyone who left her now.

"Captain," Dutch spoke, interrupted her thoughts.

"Hm? Sorry. Were you saying something?"

"Yes, Kuasa and Kamau have returned." He pointed at the two large birds in the sky.

Ivy watched as scales and feathers fell away to reveal skin and the materials of their clothes, and wings and talons turned into hands and feet.

"Kuasa, Kamau, welcome back," Ivy greeted them. "What news have you brought?"

"Nothing good," Kuasa sighed. "Tempest sold us out, and now you are to be the bride of the King of Stars and Nightmares."

"The Pale Emperor and its crew will be your dowry," said Kamau, his usually jovial face sullen with the news.

Ivy's look of surprise quickly turned to quiet rage. "When did he make this brilliant decision?"

"There was a meeting of the four kings of the sea. He refused to give the King of Stars and Nightmares back his daughter, and offered you and the Emperor in exchange and as a peace offering," Kuasa explained.

"That bastard!" Ivy said through gritted teeth. "Does he know you know?"

"I don't believe so, no."

"All right, good." Ivy chewed at her thumb as she paced.

"Captain?" asked Dutch. "What's the plan now?"

"I need to think," Ivy replied.

On the one hand, being betrothed to Donovan Doyle would get them all away from Tempest, but Doyle earned the title King of Stars and Nightmares for good reason. He would literally take a person's breath out of their lungs while his shadow paralyzed their movements just for looking at him the wrong way. People said that you would see the stars as you suffocated, even during the day. It was a horrifying experience. Doyle's temper was worse than Tempest's. Ivy had to make a choice for the sake of her and her crew's wellbeing.

"Captain?" spoke Dutch, concerned when she stopped her pacing.

She turned to Kuasa and looked the Valravn in the eyes. "I want the two of you to go back to the island and tell him I refuse to be a peace offering for his crimes."

"Captain, be reasonable," said Dutch. "This is our chance to get away from that monster."

"No, Doyle will be worse. He'll punish us all for what Tempest did, no matter what we choose. We have a better chance at survival with the devil we know," she explained.

Dutch sighed and put his hands up. "Aye, Captain." He took that moment to walk off.

Ivy knew it was a risky decision, but she had to choose the lesser of two evils. At least with Tempest they could sail freely so long as they stayed out of Doyle's territory and brought more 'toys' for Tempest to play with. She did not like trafficking others to be used and killed at Tempest's whim, but it was the only option she could see for them right now. Doyle would never let the kidnapping of his daughter go. Someone would pay for his loss. She wanted to make sure it was not her or her crew.

Tempest had her naked in his lap, her back against his chest as he ran his tongue up the side of her neck, but she barely recoiled, only shuddered. His long fingers pierced her sex, and he heard her breath catch as he added a third finger. She was not completely dry, but he wanted his cock to move more easily than it would if he took her as she was. Then again, he enjoyed hearing her scream, and blood was just as much of a lubricant to him.

Looking ahead of him, Tempest had Sang chained to the stone floor of the cave. The boy looked lifeless, but he thought he saw a hint of concern in his jewel-green eyes. Tempest's face spread with a wicked smile as he forced Sang to watch helplessly while he threw the girl to one of the many furs that lined the ground in the area he had designed for 'play'. He got on his knees and quickly grabbed her legs when she scrambled to get away from him. He flipped her on her back and heard the light crack when her head hit the ground. It was not a hard hit, but it was enough to stun her as he pulled her to him. He lined himself up at her entrance and looked up at Sang with a devilish grin as he forced himself inside of the girl in one hard thrust.

Her scream and the panicked rattle of Sang's chains were sweet sounds to him. He laughed as the girl fought him and continued to scream. Tempest put one of his hands around her throat as he viciously pumped into her, enjoying the sound of her strangled cries.

"You see, boy," he laughed, continuing to force himself deeper into her, "this is the way of the world we live in. The weak are here for the pleasures of the powerful." He pulled one of the girl's legs up and held it against his chest as he fucked and choked her just enough to keep her conscious.

He laughed even more at Sang's wide-eyed expression of horror.

"Don't pity her, this is her place in life... and your," he grinned, flipping the girl on her belly and raising her hips to take her from behind.

"Um, y-your m-majesty," came a trembling voice.

Tempest growled, throwing one hand behind him toward the frightened voice. He had an angry smile at the sound of a strangled attempt to speak.

"I thought I said not to disturb me while I'm playing with my toys," he hissed. With an exasperated sigh, he released the boy that interrupted him. "Well, what is it?" he asked impatiently, watching as the boy fell to his knees coughing up water conjured from the surrounding air. "Out with it," he snarled, raising his hand again.

The boy sputtered as he struggled to speak. "C-captain Thatch has s-sent her V-Valravn w-with a m-message."

"What. Is. It?"

As quickly as he could, he relayed Ivy's message.

Tempest growled again, pulling out of the now unconscious girl. He snapped at the guard near Sang to come gather her up and chain her back up next to the dragon. He then put his trousers back on and addressed the shaking messenger.

"Put the birds in chains and take them to my throne room. If they resist, start breaking body parts," he ordered. Tempest turned to Sang. "Don't worry, I'll be back to play with you soon." He walked out of the room, cackling.

Sang shook with the threat. He looked down at the poor girl chained beside him. She was doing about as well as he had with his 'training'. Cuts and bruises that still looked fresh covered her. That was not the first time that he had to witness her assault. She had to do the same when Tempest took him as well. They never spoke to one another, as Tempest would beat and rape them into unconsciousness. Once they were awake, it would begin again. Sometimes, Sang would die. Tempest would pull too much on his life energy, but the girl had no power to speak of that he could sense. Each session with Tempest was short for her, but she was getting weaker every time he had her.

When she stirred, Sang moved closer to her. He helped her sit up and even allowed her to lean against him for support.

"You, all right?" he tried. His English was still fairly bad, but he at least understood it better.

She groaned as she tried to get comfortable. It sounded painful. All she could do was nod slightly.

"I heal? For you?" he asked, pointing at her more minor wounds. He remembered Su Yang telling him that his saliva could heal some shallow wounds.

"You are sweet, too sweet for this place and that monster," she replied. "My name's Sinead. What's yours?"

"I am Sang," he answered. "I heal?"

"Hm? Oh! Yes, please!" She offered him her arm. "Sang? That's a funny name, i'n it?" She marveled at her arm, now covered in his spit, but healed. "How'd you do that?"

Sang though she sounded funny, like the angry man from before, but not as strong sounding. He merely shrugged at her question; he did not know how he did it either. Just that he could. They both looked up when someone came running into the room to speak with the guard that watched over them. When they left, the guard moved to unchain Sang from the floor. The guard roughly dragged him off with Sinead protesting in futility.

Upon arrival, Sang was forcefully thrown next to the large plush chair occupied by Tempest. He looked up to see Kuasa and Kamau, both on their knees, in chains.

They were both badly beaten and bleeding, Kuasa more so than Kamau.

Tempest looked over at Sang before speaking. "You see these two? This is what happens to the weak when they forget their place and disobey their betters," he explained, pointing at the twins. "Now, I would normally just dispose of them, but Ivy needs to be reminded of her place as well." He turned to the twins. "You will return to the Pale Emperor and remind Ivy of what happens when she doesn't do what she is told to." With a snap of his fingers, he ordered the release of the twins. "Fly away, little birds."

Kuasa struggled to her feet with the aid of her brother, and they both hobbled away. Sang was finally understanding the message that Tempest drilled into him daily. The world was cruel and awful, and there was only one place for those that were deemed weak or less than.

# CHAPTER 14

Ivy spotted a pair of large black birds flying towards the ship. Their flight looked off to her. One of them dropped slightly before catching themselves. And when they both landed, their usual graceful transformation was jagged and sloppy. Once in their human forms, she could see the extensive injuries they had sustained. Kuasa looked the worst.

"What the hell happened to you two?" She barely caught Kuasa when she stumbled.

"He did not accept your answer," said Kamau, coughing up blood.

"Go see Su Yang, then change back into ravens. He won't be able to heal all of your wounds," Ivy ordered, passing Kuasa over to her brother.

They both nodded, then limped off to find Su Yang.

Ivy cursed aloud. How dare that bastard hurt her people? He needed to pay for what he did to the twins, but how was she going to exact her revenge? She could not even stop him from taking Sang. What good was she as a captain if she could not protect her people? She had only one course of action.

"Set a new course," she shouted to the helmsman.

"Aye! Where to, captain?" he asked.

To their deaths, if she was not careful. "To see the King of Stars and Nightmares. We're going to the Fáinne Tromluí."

The moment she announced where they were going, she heard murmurs of discontent and unease. She was losing her crew, and all over a damn dragon whose loss she did not readily accept.

"Captain?" Dutch spoke, walking over to her. "Are you sure about this?"

In the short time Sang was on the Pale Emperor, he had made her soft, weak. Tempest had taught her to be better than that. She commanded the most powerful ship in the seas. And she would not let Tempest or any man take that from her.

"Oh, absolutely. Doyle is going to help me kill that evil bastard, and there will be no wedding," she said firmly. "We will finally be free."

"Yes, captain." Dutch bowed his head, then went off to help prepare the ship.

The Fáinne Tromluí—the nightmare ring—was a treacherous string of islands. Doyle made sure of that. No ship could pass without his knowing or without sustaining damage because of the few warships that he had heavily guarded it. Though they were likely to be expected, they were still going unannounced. She would need to cloak the ship and take a side passage to get as close as they could to the Isle of Dreams, where Doyle had his stronghold. She would need to use a lot of magic and sustain it for an extended period. For that task, she would need a lot of borrowed power. An Andr would sure have been handy for that. She just had to make do with a few of the stronger members of her crew… without killing them.

It had been a long time since someone had tried to infiltrate his stronghold without being seen, but something on the ship gave them away. Had it not been for that mistake, the Pale Emperor would have gotten to his island unscathed. The thick, rolling fog was an excellent strategy, though. He would have loved to see the look on her face when they caught her. She had the good sense to surrender without a fight, but there was no way Black Ivy Thatch came all this way to be a bride. She hated him almost as much as she hated Tempest.

"Oivy Thatch, what an unexpected pleasure ta have ye at me court," Doyle smiled, leaning forward in his chair. "Did that arse tell ye tha good news, and ye couldn't wait ta be in me bed?"

The look of utter disgust and rage on her face said everything that he wanted to know. She must have been desperate to come directly to him. The thought crossed his mind to tear her apart and send her parts along with the remains of the Pale Emperor back to Tempest, but he was too willing to give both of them up. He did not care what happened to her or her ship.

"All right, out wit it, girl. Oi want ta hear ye beg fer it," he said with a nasty grin.

"I won't beg for anything from you," she spat. "But you will help me."

"And why should Oi do a tin' like that? After all, ye are mine ta do wit as Oi please," he countered.

"Because that beast of a man has wronged us both in more ways than one, and he is going to get what's coming to him," she said. "Question is, do you want him dead as bad as I do?"

"O' course Oi do, but Oi ain't willin' ta start a war fer it."

"Well, I am. Your daughter's still alive, by the way," she added.

He eyed her with some suspicion as he leaned back in his chair. Even if she was telling the truth, his daughter would not be the happy, foul-mouthed little girl he knew. Still, he was not about to let her die at the hands of that animal, either. He wanted his little girl back, no matter what condition her mind was likely in. It was his fault that she was in that situation in the first place. Had he not sent for her, she would still be safe with his sister in the colonies in America, but he wanted to be a proper father to her.

"All right, Oi'll help ye, but ye need ta bring me back me Sinead first. Once she's safe, Oi'll help ye kill yer beast," he offered.

"I'll need at least two of your ships and strong fighters if I'm going to get her out alive."

He grinned. "Anytin' fer me blushin' bride," he laughed with a wink. "Now, be on yer way. Save me li'l girl."

Ivy gave a curt nod, then turned to leave, but Doyle saw the fierceness in her eyes. She was an exquisite and powerful woman, brazen thing that she was. He felt a stirring within him he had not felt since Aine. While Ivy may not have wanted to marry him, perhaps she would want a go in the sack before she left. Not wanting to spoil his mood with more words, he got up and grabbed her arm before she got too far. He spun her around and kissed her hard, holding her in a tight embrace. To his surprise, she kissed him back.

She broke their kiss. "This means nothing. I'm not marrying you. I will never belong to you or anyone else."

"Fine, fine. Oi just want a good fuck, is all," he replied.

She looked at him with hooded eyes. "I should warn you that I bite."

A low growl cleared his throat before he captured her lips with his again. He quickly broke their kiss to remove her blouse and tight leather trousers. After taking a few moments to admire her nearly pristine white skin, slightly tinted pink with the heat of her arousal, he lifted her up and sat her in his chair. He dropped to his knees and slid hers apart, revealing, for the first time to him, the heart of her desire. The pink flesh of her sex was swollen with need. She jumped when his thumb circled her clit. He wondered for a second if his hand was cold. He pinched her little bud, making her wiggle in her seat, but then she arched into his rough touch.

"Oi'll fuck ye wit me tongue until ye beg fer me cock," he said, trailing a line of kisses up the inside of her soft thigh, slick with her arousal.

"I don't be—by the gods!" she shouted as the velvet feel of his tongue ran along the center of her entrance.

With a grin, his mouth covered her sex as he murmured, "Damn right." He sucked on her lips before his broad tongue licked at her core, the tip of it rounding her slit before it dipped inside, working tirelessly to make her cry out.

"Gods, please," she panted, digging her hand into his short, black hair, grabbing fistfuls like a madwoman.

He groaned, pulling her closer to the edge of the seat, and buried his face deeper between her thighs, devouring her so completely that all she could do was moan and cry out to the gods. He chuckled when her walls flexed and spasmed with the onset of release.

Pulling back, he looked up at her flushed face and smiled. "Now, beg."

"Never," she breathed ruefully.

He thought he heard her whimper when he stood back up to take off his shirt. "Ye sure about that?" he asked, a smirk on his face as he slowly undid his trousers, pulling out his hardened length. Stroking himself lightly, he could see the hunger in her eyes as he got closer.

Her breathing grew more labored before her fingers found their way into her hole, soaked with unfulfilled need. He grabbed her wrist and removed her hand to place it around his own throbbing desire. That prompted her to get on her knees in front of him. She slowly ran her wicked tongue up the underside of his cock from base to tip. He threw his head back, his eyes slamming shut as she lapped up the clear bead that leaked out of the opening of his crown. His fingers slid into her hair, urging her to take more of him in. She smiled up at him before her small mouth opened to take him, her lips straining to get around the girth of him.

"Fuck," he growled out as her tongue swept the wide flare of the head. It was all he could do not to fuck the back of her throat.

Her mouth was so warm and wet that it nearly killed him to pull her off him. She looked up at him, confusion on her face as she wiped her mouth.

"All right, ye win."

She smiled again, sitting on the floor, spreading her legs and exposing herself to him. Leaning back on one hand, she beckoned him down with her. He was all too happy to oblige her. He mounted her, bringing his head down to kiss her as he positioned the head of his prick at her entrance. His mouth hovered over hers, his breath catching the moment he entered her. Again, he swore. She felt too good.

Doyle did not know how much time had passed, nor did he care as he lay sprawled on the fur that covered a large part of the floor. It had been far too long since someone fucked him that well. He sat up to watch Ivy as she dressed. He smiled back at her when she turned briefly over her shoulder with a smile. When she went to leave, he caught her wrist.

"When ye get back, Oi'll put in a good word wit tha other sea kings ta see about ye takin' Tempest's place."

She snatched her wrist away. "I didn't fuck you for all that."

"Oi know, but ye'd be a better king than him, and tha King of Storms could use tha company. So could Oi."

She smirked. "I appreciate the offer, but that title comes with too many rules, and I like my freedom far too much."

He returned her smirk with one of his own. "All right, then. Be on yer way," he said, waving her off. "Be careful, Oivy."

She was gone before he could say anything more. He briefly wondered if she had put a spell on him. Dhampir had that ability, and she was half succubus. He shook the strange line of thoughts from his head. He could not lose focus. Not over a woman, not again. Especially when Alexander Tempest was involved. He could not allow himself to get attached again. Though he knew she was an excellent fighter, Tempest was still a formidable king of the sea, and there was always the chance that he would kill Ivy for what she was going to do.

# CHAPTER 15

There were so many bodies surrounding her, the sounds of gunfire and fighting made her ears ring. She looked around the beach. So many men and women came charging out of nowhere the moment they hit land. Doyle had allotted her two of his sloops with enough men to help her fight and cover her escape. They were not supposed to know that they were coming, but they did. Somehow, they found out. There was still a spy on her ship, and they got to Tempest before she could. Now Ivy and her crew, along with Doyle's men, were at Tempest's mercy. All who remained alive were captured and brought to his cave of horrors to be dealt with.

Tempest had joined the fight on the beach. Blood covered him, but none of it was his. As far as she could tell, there was not a scratch on him. He had a cruel smile on his face as he ascended his throne.

"Ivy, how good of you to come see me again," he started. "It was a very foolish thing for you to do, though."

"How?" she asked behind gritted teeth.

"How what?" He sat down as he wiped the blood from his face with a rag.

She merely continued to glare at him. He knew exactly what she wanted to know.

"Oh! That. Well, Kuasa and Kamau aren't the only shapeshifters on your crew," he explained, then waved someone over.

A boy with short, blond hair came out of the shadows, a Cheshire grin on his tanned face.

"Tommy?" she said in surprise. "Tommy isn't a shapeshifter."

"No," started the boy, "but I am."

The boy's skin rippled. Tanned skin fell away, revealing pale flesh. His chest grew into two good sized spheres, long arms and legs became shorter and more feminine, and his clothes were suddenly loose.

"Lizzy," Ivy snarled. "What did you do to Tommy?"

"The boy? Oh, I killed him months ago," she grinned as she happily plopped down into Tempest's lap.

"No wonder your crew has lost respect for you. You didn't even notice the change," Tempest laughed.

"I'll kill you both!" Ivy roared, but Tempest had her and what remained of her crew chained up.

"You have two choices now, Ivy: either do as you were told and marry Doyle, or I can put you back in my harem and find a replacement for the captain of the Emperor," he offered. "The second option would be best, honestly. You could use more training. Might humble you a bit more."

"I'll never go back to your bed," she spat. "I'd rather die."

Tempest's smile broadened as he snapped his fingers. Two guards came out from behind his throne. One pulled Sang along, and the other had a limp body. The one with the body threw it at her feet. When the body landed and rolled over, Ivy covered her mouth to stifle a gasp. It was Sinead, her body a sickly color and waterlogged.

"You sure death is what you want?" Tempest asked, amused. "Because that would suit me just fine." He removed Lizzy from his lap, much to her displeasure, and got up and stepped over Sinead's body. He grabbed Ivy by the face and squeezed hard. She struggled against him, grabbing his arm to remove his hand.

"I gave you everything, and this is what I get in return? A mutiny?" He brought her closer and scented the air around her. He growled low in his chest. "You fucked him? Doyle?"

He threw her to the ground and roared. It was a demonic sound followed by heavy breathing, and then a maniacal laugh. Ivy watched as spikes broke through the flesh of his brow near his hairline. Small spikes grew into long horns that curved around his ears from behind. His already long fingers extended further into long talons, and his skin turned a sickly blue. A spaded tail whipped behind him as his laugh turned into a demonic growl. He looked otherworldly and frightening. His teeth were rows of shark-like points when he smiled menacingly down at her.

"I'm going to make you regret letting him soil you," he said through his fangs.

He sent her flying a fair distance when he backhanded her. Ivy hit the ground hard when she landed on the jagged stone floor of the cave. She weakly sat up and touched the side of her face that hit and drew blood. It had been a long time since she had seen him so mad that he transformed, but he was not the only demon in the room. She got to her feet as he stalked over to her. Her skin paled even more with a gray tint to it. She saw him stop when her newly formed talons wrapped around the chains between her wrists and pulled them taut until they broke apart. Hissing behind her fangs, she crouched low, and then charged at him. She was going to wipe that smug look off his face.

With her claws, she swiped at him, driving him backwards. His tail caught her by the leg and sent her back to the ground, but she recovered quickly, and sprang backwards on her hands. Again, she ran at him at full speed. Dodging his fists, she slid past him and caught his tail, ripping it out of him with such force that he roared in pain and fell to his knees. Ivy took the dismembered tail and wrapped it around his throat from behind. He stood with her on his back as she strangled him backwards until she was on her feet again. She pulled as tight as she could, listening to him choke. She put her foot into the small of his back and pulled harder until he was back on his knees. His horns retracted back into his skull, and his blue skin turned back to its normal translucent white as she guided him to the ground. She had finally done it. She killed her demon.

Sang looked on as Ivy left Tempest on the ground. She walked back towards those that were in chains so that she could release them. She looked up at him standing next to the throne, but his attention turned to Tempest, who was now standing behind her with a malevolent look in his wild eyes. He did not turn back into his demonic form, but he did not seem to need to. Sang watched as Tempest grabbed a fistful of her hair and slammed her hard on the ground. Sang heard the crack of her skull as it hit, but still she moved, fought back after having the wind knocked out of her. Her movements were sluggish and sloppy. Tempest only laughed.

Sang continued to watch, unphased, as Tempest beat Ivy senseless. No one came to her aid, and he did not blame them. Tempest was a beast of a man, and he showed no remorse for his actions. Any that got in his way was as good as dead. This was the way of things. This was going to be his life. Sang frowned at the thoughts. He did not owe Ivy anything after she turned him over to Tempest, but he did not want a life of abuse and unending death. He looked at the guard at his side, transfixed by the violence, then back at Ivy. Her eyes were empty, and her life was fading fast as she choked on the water collected from the air around them. Tempest had her up in the air with a gesture of his hand. Sang knew that feeling all too well, drowning in the air. He did not like that feeling.

The guard went down quickly and quietly to Sang's surprise. He was a large man, and his blood, thick and foul tasting as it was, gifted Sang with the strength he would need. He still could not get out of his chains. They differed from the others, stronger, and they still burned his skin, but he could summon his fire. He shot a ball of electric green flames at Tempest's back. When he turned angrily to look, Sang was already beside him. Sang swiped at Tempest with his right hand, purposefully missing, and immediately went down on his hands to the right and brought his right leg up to strike Tempest in the head. Tempest went down hard and fast, and much to Sang's delight, he stayed down. Sang gathered an unconscious Ivy up from the ground where Tempest had dropped her when Sang attacked him with fire.

Sang had seen enough abuse in his brief life. It had become clear to him that cruelty was the true language of the world. He would remind Ivy of that later... if she lived. When he left the cave with Ivy in his arms and what remained of her captured crew behind him, no one stopped them. In fact, they parted out of his way and let them all leave. Now, he was the monster they feared.

# CHAPTER 16

When Ivy regained consciousness, she looked into Sang's eyes as he stared down at her. There was a coldness to them now, and they were dull, darkened by violence and abuse. She had failed him, and yet, he still saved her. While she could, she gave the order to collect Sinead's body and re-board the ship. Su Yang and a few others had stayed with the ship to keep it ready for when they returned. She had hoped that they would have gotten Sinead out alive, and that nearly half of her crew were not dead, but Tempest had been defeated. She had seen the fire coming before she had blacked out. Sang had taken him down when she could not. Ivy had felt unfit as captain of the Pale Emperor. Once she got her strength back, she would resign. Though she was not sure who would take her place. Dutch had died in the ambush on the beach. At least he died without witnessing her epic failure in killing Tempest herself.

The remaining crew that stayed with the ship and those with minor injuries followed her orders to sail back to the nightmare ring. She would have them dock on an island within the ring and rest up. Ivy asked Kuasa and Kamau to take Sinead's body back to Doyle and to come back as soon as possible. She did not want them hurt again for delivering the wrong news again. Once they were done with that task, she would dissolve their contract, freeing them once and for all. They would likely argue with her about it. They had grown quite attached to her, but it needed to be done so they could live better lives.

After giving Su Yang the order to tend to the wounded and leave her for last, she allowed Sang to put her in her bed. She accepted his offer to heal what he could, but she wanted to be alone after that. Her pride and ego suffered alongside her body.

As he laid her down to rest, he thought he caught sight of a tear falling down her cheek. Perhaps he had been too rough with how he healed her minor wounds, but he doubted it. She was weak, but not when it came to physical pain. Tempest had definitely humbled her. Ivy was not nearly as strong as he thought she was. He pitied her for how visibly weak she was. He refused to be the same.

After leaving the captain's quarters, Sang went back to see Su Yang. He offered to help him with the minor wounds of the crew.

"I appreciate the help, but I do not want you ingesting any of their blood by mistake. Your saliva turns acidic for a short period after you have had blood."

Sang nodded in acknowledgement, then went to the drawer he remembered Su Yang keeping the acupuncture charts in. He would study those instead, since he could not help. As he reviewed the scrolls, he felt he was being watched.

"I sense that there is a change within you, Sang. I can see it in your eyes, an imbalance," Su Yang explained.

"What is imbalance? I do not understand."

Su Yang smiled wryly. "I see your English has improved some."

"What is imbalance?"

Su Yang straightened up. Sang heard it in his own voice, the demand for an answer.

"There is darkness inside you now. You have known great pain and suffering. Your heart is not the same," Su Yang tried.

Sang still did not understand completely, but he recognized the change in himself.

"You will need to fix the imbalance before the darkness consumes you."

Sang stared at him blankly for a moment. He did not understand what the doctor was telling him, and he did not care anymore. He went back to studying and memorizing the scrolls.

"You were not the first dragon on this ship," Su Yang said, interrupting his studying.

Sang sighed with exasperation before putting the charts down. Something was on Su Yang's mind, and he wanted Sang to listen.

"He did not like ships either, and he too was imbalanced like you," Su Yang started. "Raesh was different from other Andr, also like you."

Su Yang told Sang about the other imbalanced Andr named Raesh, and how close he and Ivy were. He did not go too much into detail about their relationship, but he was not supposed to tell Sang about the other dragon. If he wanted more answers, he would have to get them out of Ivy. For now, he would continue to watch the doctor as he treated the crew members that passed through, and he would continue to study his charts.

Ivy had just entered a deep sleep when Sang came back to her room. She could tell it was late, but it confused her that he was there. There was no emotion in his vacant eyes when he brought her back to the ship. She realized he had no affection for her anymore. If he ever did.

"Is something wrong?" she asked, wincing when she sat up.

He sat down on the bed next to her and calmly asked, "What is Raesh?"

Shit. Su Yang must have finally told him. "Who," she corrected. "Who was Raesh."

"Who is Raesh?" he asked again, more firmly.

Ivy saw a mix of impatience and ire in his dark green eyes. She was reluctant, but she supposed he deserved to know about his predecessor.

"Raesh was an Andr, but you probably already knew that much," she started, trying and failing to get comfortable.

His face scrunched up in confusion. "What Raesh mean?" he asked.

She regarded him thoughtfully for a moment before answering. "Resurrecting darkness, in some ancient language that Andr spoke," she explained. "He and I were lovers. Tempest found him when he was younger than you. We grew up together on that island in his harem." She sighed with the memory. This was going to be hard for her, but Sang wanted, no, needed, to know. "Raesh was used to train me when I came into my powers at sixteen. He had looked older than me, and he had some skill, but I knew he was closer to my age. Tempest liked to watch us sometimes, just to make sure I was good enough for him to take over. I'm only half succubus, and unlike Tempest, I can't kill through sex, but I can induce madness because of the addiction to sex with me. My lovers eventually die over time from my feedings, but not for a while."

She watched him for any kind of reaction, but saw none. However, he fixated on her and listened attentively.

"When I got command of the Emperor, I begged Tempest to let him join my crew. Raesh was strong, aggressive, and when Tempest wasn't fucking the life out of him, he was his enforcer. I didn't want that life for him anymore, and thankfully, Tempest got bored with him and let me take him." She paused a few moments. She was not sure if she should continue. The wheels were turning in his head, and she could see him contemplating something. When she went to touch his arm, she drew her hand back immediately from the look he gave her.

He did not recoil from her. There was only that look. As if she was beneath him and not allowed to touch him. It hurt her more than she thought it would, but she knew she deserved that look. She disgusted him.

Sang looked at her with contempt in his eyes. He was nothing more than a replacement for someone else. She never actually cared about him. No wonder it was so easy for her to hand him over to Tempest. The thought crossed his mind to slit her throat and be done with her, but he was not ready just yet.

"Where Raesh?" he asked, keeping calm.

"Hm?" she asked, wide-eyed.

He cleared his throat. "Where is Raesh?"

She lowered her gaze before answering. "He died," she mumbled.

"How?"

He noticed her reluctance to answer, so he got up and disrobed. When he climbed back into her bed, he caught her and pinned her down when she tried to move away. He had her firmly pinned beneath him, and still she struggled, but did not call out for help.

"How?" he growled. "How did he die?"

She stared wide-eyed up at him. He could see the fear in her eyes, but her body betrayed her. When he parted her legs with his knee and rubbed it against her cunt, he could feel how wet she was. He could smell her arousal, and he heard the sharp intake of air when his knee touched her most sensitive part. It excited him, and he would be lying to himself if he thought otherwise, but a low voice in his head told him to stop. He did not want to listen.

He dipped his head down and ran his tong along the side of her neck before whispering in her ear, "Tell me," in a low growl.

"I killed him," she replied after a moment.

"Why?" he asked, putting both her hands into one of his. He needed one hand free to wipe away the tear that had fallen down her cheek. "Why did you kill?"

"I had to. He was going to kill Tempest."

Her answer confused him. He thought she hated Tempest. "Why?" he asked again, his frustration showing.

"Because Tempest was stronger. Raesh could never beat him, and I would have lost him. Tempest would have taken him from me. I did it to protect him."

So that was it. He had his answer.

"I didn't know he wouldn't come back," she sobbed.

He sighed in exasperation, then roughly grabbed her by the throat. "Stop crying," he commanded.

"Please," she squeaked out.

He was feeling conflicted now. She killed her dragon lover to protect him from a monster, but he never resurrected. He did not understand that. He had died many times and always came back. What made Raesh's last death permanent? What did she do to him? Should he kill her so she could not do the same to him? Many questions plagued him as his grip tightened on her throat, then something snapped in his head and the voice screaming at him to stop hurting her quieted down, and the questions stopped. He released her throat.

"Do you want me?" he asked plainly.

There was confusion in her fearful eyes now.

"Answer me," he ordered, tightening his grip again. His knee found her again when she did not answer right away.

"Yes," she wheezed.

He smiled down at her, then removed his hand from her throat. His hand slid its way down her throat and onto her chest. He palmed her breast, just as he had been taught to do with Sinead, pinching the rosy pink bud between his fingers. Again, he smiled as she arched into his hand and against his knee.

"No, not yet," he said. "Be patient." His mouth descended onto her breast, and he wrapped his tongue around her erect nipple before pulling it between his teeth.

She hissed, then let out a sigh. He chuckled at the sounds as his hand glided down her flat stomach and continued its journey until it reached the warmth of her sex. Releasing her breast, he looked up at her as his middle finger dipped inside of her. Once more, she arched into his hand, his thumb rubbing her clit in maddening circles.

"You listen, yes?" he asked, grinning as he continued to stroke her core.

She moaned and nodded her head the best she could. His left hand still had her arms pinned down.

"Good. I stay with you, you teach me."

She shook her head, whimpering when he took his hand away.

"I stay with you, you teach me," he repeated, cupping her mound as he drove two fingers inside of her.

"All right," she cried out.

He knew he was hurting her, and she was still injured, but that did not matter to him. "Good. You are weak, but I will make strong again," he smiled devilishly, kissing her fiercely before she could object. He spread her legs farther apart, and with his hand, positioned himself at her entrance. "You must heal now," he said, easing himself inside her slowly and enjoying the feel of her walls tightening around him, welcoming him in.

He released her wrists once he was sure she would not run or fight him. She wrapped her arms around his neck as he lifted her legs to gain deeper access to her. When he grew bored with that position, he pulled out of her. He laughed when she protested, but he turned her over onto her stomach and pulled her back onto his waiting cock. His thrusts were hard, but he kept a steady rhythm. He wanted her to last. While on his knees, he pulled her up, her back against his chest. He continued to pump into her, making her cry out as he cupped her breasts and lightly bit into her shoulder. She panted and moaned, and he soon felt her pull on his life force. It was not a strong pull, not at all like Tempest's. He grunted and growled as he pumped harder, trying to shake the awful memories from his thoughts. His focus needed to be on her.

Once he no longer felt the pull on his energy, he released her. She fell onto the bed in a heap, breathing hard, but he was not done with her. Not yet. He did not have his release.

# Chapter 17

A few days had passed since the failed raid and rescue on Tempest's island. Ivy and Sang had spent the bulk of it locked in her quarters. The wounded crew was on the mend, some fully healed. All notions she had of stepping down as captain were now removed. Sang had demanded that she remain the captain of the Pale Emperor, and that he would kill anyone that disobeyed her orders. She was not all together sure how she felt about that. She did not believe in running her ship with an iron fist, but after recent events, she would have to for a while.

The ship was still in good shape and ready to sail again. They had heard nothing from Doyle, and he made no attempt to retaliate for his daughter's death. It was time to go, but Ivy was enjoying her time in bed with Sang. He had licked every inch of her, marking every part of her as his. Tempest had taught him things she did not think were possible, and she felt a little bad about it. She knew how that sort of training went with Tempest. At least something good came from it, though. She would have to teach him to be a bit more gentle and less selfish as a lover.

"Ship!"

She heard someone call out. It sounded like Kamau. The sound of cannons soon followed the call going off and gunfire. Shortly after, they heard panicked cries. They were under attack. Ivy and Sang quickly dressed as the ship rocked, but the ship was not being hit. The bulk of the crew was on the beach. By the time she and Sang had arrived, there were bodies in every direction. She had given the order to return fire while still on the ship, but it was too late for some of those camped out on the beach. There was already not much left of her crew, but what remained was still willing to fight. It was hard to tell whose ship it was until she saw Jack smiling beside a tall, pale man with a look of rage in his eyes. Tempest was still alive, and he had found them. Ivy cursed, then went to prepare herself for a fight.

He did not wait for the ship to get closer, and she watched as he called for a small wave to carry him ashore. He stepped off of the wave, drawing two blades from his sides the moment his feet touched land. Ivy watched as he carved a bloody path towards her, his blades darting between the ribs and collar bones of her men like a pair of shears cutting through cloth. His eyes never left hers as he continued his warpath. Kuasa and Kamau were too busy fighting their own battles, but they were fairing well enough against the small group that surrounded them. Ivy was on her own for the fight to come. She readied her own sword, then marched a steady pace at her target. She would not hide from him.

Before they could meet, a blur of pale skin and black hair ran past her directly at Tempest. She watched as Sang pushed Tempest away with a solid front kick to his chest. When Tempest recovered and tried to rush him, Sang quickly went down on one hand to Tempest's right and brought his legs up, putting Tempest back on the ground with a knee to the chest and a foot to the head with one leg. Sang stood confidently back on his feet while Tempest spat out blood to the side before wiping his mouth as he glared up at Sang. Sang's boldness surprised

Ivy, but she was familiar with the look in Tempest's eyes. Before she could call out to him, get him to move away, it was already too late. It looked so out of place yet fit so well with the look of wide-eyed horror frozen on Sang's face. The blue veins that ran through his body stood out even more as they bulged beneath his skin. She watched him fall, the bloody point of an icicle sticking out of his chest as it impaled and pushed out his still-beating heart. The bright green flames licked and devoured his flesh, ashes falling to the bloodied sand like snow, followed by a man-shaped husk. Her dragon was dead.

Though she knew Sang would reform, there was always that chance that he would not... like Raesh. Kuasa and Kamau were still fighting their group, and even Su Yang had joined the fray, transforming into a large gray wolf to join the other monsters on the field. Ivy was on her own to fight her monster. She watched Tempest rise from the ground, the glint of sunlight reflecting off his blades. The sound of her own blood rushing with adrenaline filled her ears with the metallic scent of fresh blood and the smell of burned flesh filling her nose.

"Don't worry, Ivy. I won't do that to you. I like my meat tender enough to fall off the bone," he purred, coming towards her.

The bitter taste of bile hit the back of her throat as she readied herself for attack, but she would not let fear get in her way. She would show him who Ivy Thatch really was.

He awoke to the sounds of metal against metal, men and women screaming and fighting, and the sounds of bones against bones. The smell of ash, blood, and gunpowder filled his nostrils, but what he saw made his breath catch, all his senses zeroing in on Ivy as she floated a few feet from the ground. Multiple cuts left her bleeding badly, with bruises forming on her fair skin. She clawed helplessly at her throat and chest, choking and trying to spit out water. Below her lay a body contorted in ways that there was no way it could still function, with tiny red spikes sticking out of every part. He looked at the face, completely twisted in pain. It was Kuasa, and Kamau was nowhere to be found.

Sang knew he had to help somehow. Tempest looked like Ivy gave almost as good as she got. He was drowning her slowly for it. Sang grabbed a man that was going through with a sword and making sure anyone on Ivy's crew were dead, and the sound of tearing flesh was in his ears with the taste of warm, coppery blood going over his tongue and down his throat. The moment he tried to summon his fire, very little appeared. It was not enough to help her. He watched as her arms fell limp to her sides; her legs dangled lifelessly as she hung in the air. The light was fading in her eyes when Tempest suddenly dropped her. Before that, Sang had heard a single shot. It hit Tempest on the shoulder.

Tempest grunted in pain as he held his shoulder and angrily looked behind him. Sang took the chance and quickly recovered Ivy away from Tempest. The funny sounding angry man and what looked to be a shadow had attacked Tempest. While Tempest was being engaged, Sang tried to heal Ivy's wounds, but his saliva burned her. He remembered what Su Yang had said about that too late, but the pain his saliva caused made Ivy cough up water and blood as she howled out. Kamau had returned, flying in at their side. When he changed into his human form, Sang saw the damage that had been done to him, but Kamau appeared indifferent to his wounds. He just shook as he stared at Kuasa's mangled corpse. Kamau was useless as he was, and for once, Sang wanted to fight. He gave the barely breathing Ivy to the grief-stricken Kamau, then go up to join the fight between Tempest and the man he assumed was the King of Stars and Nightmares that Ivy had mentioned the night before. Donovan Doyle, Sinead's father.

Before Sang could jump in to help, Doyle had Tempest on his knees, pulling the air out of his lungs, but Tempest was not down yet. Doyle could barely stand as Tempest was pulling his blood out through his skin in the form of spikes. Sang wanted to help, but when he threw a large ball of fire at Tempest, the strange sentient shadow chose that moment to get in the way. Doyle fell to his knees, a vacant look in his eyes as the shadow let out an ear-piercing screech as it flailed about until it disappeared. All that remained was a scorch mark on the ground. Tempest fell forward on his hands, gasping for air. Sang looked at Doyle, who was slumped over and swaying side to side. Tempest struggled to his feet, grabbing a sword as he did. He stood behind Doyle, still breathing hard, and pulled Doyle's head back by his hair. Tempest slowly dragged the blade across Doyle's throat.

Doyle's body fell to the side when Tempest pushed him down, then Tempest turned to Sang, who was in shock from what he had done. His eyes went in and out of focus, his breath came out in quick heavy bursts, and a strange smell entered his nose. He shook as Tempest came at him, but he could not move. What did he do? He vaguely felt the slash of steel across his chest, followed by something warm and wet. Why did he not just let Doyle fight alone? Why did he have to help? What kind of monster helped the person who hurt them? Question after question ran through his mind until his muscles contracted at the feeling of something sharp going through his abdomen. Something inside his mind snapped as he looked down to see that he had been run through with a sword. He growled when he looked up at Tempest, smiling as he forced the blade through further. Sang grabbed the blade of the sword with his bare hands, pulling it out as he moved backwards, all while glaring at Tempest. Tempest kept pushing the sword forward, preventing Sang from coming free of it. Sang tightened his grip, cutting deeper into his palms, then set the sword on fire, forcing Tempest to let go and step back.

With a shaky hand, Sang removed the sword and threw it to the ground. With a shaky hand, Sang removed the sword and threw it to the ground. He could feel rage contorting his face as he stared at Tempest, all while holding the wound in his gut. His look of rage turned to one of glee when he saw the look on Tempest's face as he cauterized the wound with one hand and conjured a large flame around the fist of the other. He punched the air in Tempest's direction, sending the ball of fire directly at him. Tempest could barely dodge it, Sang's lip curled in response. With both shoulders wounded, Tempest charged Sang, but Sang moved faster, ducking and dodging each of Tempest's punches with moderate ease. Sang hit Tempest in the stomach, sending him back several feet. Tempest roared in anger, then charged into his demonic form.

Sang did not understand why Tempest did not just use his elemental powers on him, but he was not about to remind him of them. He saw the wounds in Tempest's shoulders heal, and he moved faster than before. Sang kicked sand up into Tempest's eyes when he got close, then twisted his body and brought the heel of his left foot across Tempest's face. Tempest went down hard, and before he could get back up, Sang got behind him. He grabbed a fistful of Tempest's hair and pulled his head back. Sang reared his head back before he bent down and sank his fangs deep into Tempest's exposed throat, releasing a large amount of his venom. When he released him, Tempest wavered, and then fell to the ground. Sang watched as he twitched and convulsed and then went still.

Though he was sure he was dead, Sang did not want to take any chances. He dragged Tempest's body towards the sea, then threw him in. He watched as the water consumed the body, pulling it under, then turned his attention to what remained of Tempest's crew. In their panic, they all fled back to their ship as Sang lobbed multiple green balls of fire at them. Sang stopped his barrage and waited until the ship was far enough away from the shore. The sloop was pretty fast, getting a fair distance away, but not far enough away fast enough. Sang spread his arms wide, then brought them forward, sending a massive flame rapidly at the ship. He saw a few of them jump off the ship before the flame hit, but the fire spread quickly and those left on board screamed as they burned. He laughed manically when some tried to put the fire out by jumping into the sea, but his flames were not so easily extinguished. The screams continued until the ship eventually exploded. Sang laughed and laughed, falling to his knees as his laughter turned into tears and cries of anguish. He held his head and howled in pain, then collapsed.

When Sang woke up, he noticed he was not where he fell. He was back on the Pale Emperor and tucked into a bed.

"You have awakened! I was worried that you would not," spoke Su Yang.

Sang turned to see the old man. Su Yang looked in poor shape. His left arm was in a sling, he was missing his right eye, and he was bandaged up.

"Do not move too much," he said. "You have been asleep for four days."

Sang ignored the doctor's orders and sat up, anyway. He immediately regretted doing so. The room spun around and would not stop until he laid back down.

"I warned you," Su Yang laughed before going into a coughing fit.

Sang waited for him to calm down before speaking. "Where is Ivy?"

Su Yang raised a curious brow. He took a moment before answering, as if he was uncertain he should say. "The captain is in her quarters resting, as you should be."

Sang once again ignored Su Yang and struggled out of the bed and stumbled out of the door, ignoring the calls for him to come back. He needed to see her for himself. He passed by Kamau, who walked about absently with a vacant look on his face, but Sang did not have the energy to talk to him. Nor did he have the desire to stop him from throwing himself overboard. He would ask about that later... maybe. Perhaps someone should have kept watch over him, but it was late and what few remained were busy healing or working.

He made it to Ivy's quarters to find her in bed with another man. The other man got out from under Ivy quickly as Sang approached. Sang glared at him until he bolted for the door. He turned his attention back to Ivy, who wrapped herself in the blanket and tried to look as small as possible, with her eyes peering at him over her knees. Sang found the behavior to be curious. Why was she so afraid of him? When he sat next to her, she shrank back from his touch. He withdrew his hand and asked her why she feared him so. He was genuinely confused, and a touch concerned.

"You don't remember? You set a ship full of people on fire and laughed about it like a madman. And you killed Doyle when you set his set his shadow on fire."

"I was helping," he tried.

"So was he. You helped Tempest just so you could kill him yourself."

Sang had no memory of killing Tempest or setting a ship on fire. He shook the more he tried to remember, then everything came flooding back to him all at once. What had he done to those people? Why did their cries of pain bring him so much joy? What kind of monster was he now? He was so engrossed in his own panic that Ivy might as well have been under water calling out to him.

When she lightly touched his arm and called his name again, all his shaking ceased instantly.

"Sang?" she tried again.

His face went cold, emotionless, as he turned to her. He smiled wickedly and said, "Call me, Raesh."

# ABOUT THE AUTHOR

Ember Drake is an American author from Columbia, South Carolina, who now lives in Georgia with her younger sister. At ten, she started writing and has aspired to be a published author ever since. Ember has always had a love of dragons and wolves. Jokingly, she was told that all she needed was to put them together and then she would be happy. As a result, Ember created Raesh, who she modeled after her favorite former Power Ranger, Johnny Yong Bosch. She modeled Roland/Zaven after her favorite actor, Matt Ryan.

She had been working the House of Ausher series since the age of seventeen when it was just three short stories that only included vampires and werewolves, both of which she is a huge fan of. The series evolved from terrible Backstreet Boys fan fiction about three brothers to what it is today.